Fueled By Flames

Hidden Realms of Silver Lake
Book 9

Vella Day

Fueled By Flames
Copyright © 2020 by Vella Day
Print Edition
www.velladay.com
velladayauthor@gmail.com

Cover Art by Jaycee DeLorenzo
Edited by Rebecca Cartee and Carol Adcock-Bezzo

Published in the United States of America
Print book ISBN: 978-1-951430-03-0

What would you do if you found out the man who is hotter than sin has been lying to you?

Dragon Shifter, Tory Sinclair, wants to believe the Fey, Kenton Forrester, is a good guy, but how can she? He convinced her whole family to keep secrets from her. Sure, he and his family have helped her siblings many times, but lying goes against every fiber of her being.

Only after the deaths of four successful locals do Tory and the other Guardians realize the only one who can help them is Kenton. Now that stinks.

Kenton has messed up royally. Tory is his mate, and yet she doesn't want much to do with him. He's kept a low profile for weeks, but now it's time to make his move—but will it be the right one? Forgiveness will be the hardest battle he's ever had to face—and that includes fighting a few demons along the way.

Chapter One

"I CAN'T DO this anymore." Kenton Forrester's anxiety was already at an all-time high, and something had to give. Considering Feys were supposed to be calm under all circumstances, avoiding Tory Sinclair wasn't helping his mental state.

After his brother placed the last dish in the cupboard of the house they shared, he spun around. "Can't do what?" Bevon asked, acting all innocent.

His brother knew. Kenton had been going on and on about Tory for weeks. "You know what. I can't seem to stay away from Tory."

The left side of his brother's lips quirked upward. "I still don't know why you're avoiding her. She's your mate. I say go for it, big brother."

"And how do you propose I do that? Teleport to the middle of her jewelry store showroom and say, *Excuse me, miss, you don't know me, but I was the one who saved your life over a month ago, and then erased your memory after whisking you off to an unknown realm.*"

Bevon grinned. "That could work."

"Somehow, I don't think that will endear her to me." Kenton pointed a finger at his brother. "Then I'll add, *And did I mention I made your whole family promise to never tell you what really happened after you were infected by that dark Fey?*"

Bevon just shook his head. "Self-pity is as an ugly trait as sarcasm. Get over yourself. Do what everyone else does. Bump into her at a bar or on the street and introduce yourself. Oh wait. I forgot. You don't go out."

"Shut up." It didn't matter that his brother made a valid point.

Bevon moved closer. "I get it will be hard for you, but you can do this. Use your charm to get her to go out with you. And by charm, I don't mean your magic."

"Easier said than done." Kenton had no idea why this was stressing him out. He was hundreds of years old and had dated many women in his realm. On Feyrion, everyone knew he was next in line to be the king, so finding a woman to fawn over him was easy. But here? On foreign soil? Not so much.

"Just talk to her. I'm not suggesting you lie to her about her past. Far from it. I'm merely saying not to put all of your cards on the table on the first date. Bit by bit, let her know the danger she was in after her attack. You can then tell her the lengths you had to go to save her."

For once, his brother made sense. "That's actually a good idea."

Bevon hopped up on the kitchen counter, clearly enjoying being able to give advice for a change. "I know it is. On Feyrion, Tory seemed like a sweet girl, one who was the forgiving type."

"You barely saw her."

He shrugged. "I dropped by the Royal Castle a few times when she was healing from her deathly experience."

"Tory was mostly out of it."

"Not that last day. She was up and about. We spoke a bit. I got a good feeling about her. From what I could tell, Tory is a strong, independent woman, but she also has a kind and understanding nature to her."

He'd thought the same thing. Kenton studied his brother—as in the one who had little to no restraint when it came to women or anything else in his life. "Let me ask you this: Have you ever asked out a woman from Tarradon—one who had no idea you're a Fey from nobility?"

"No, why would I when there are plenty of Feys and Fairies in Feyrion who want me?"

"That's what I thought." His brother was a hopeless playboy and not someone Kenton should be taking any dating advice from. He pulled open the refrigerator to look for something to eat. Not that he couldn't swipe a hand and create some gourmet masterpiece, but he was trying to learn to live in Tarradon, as backward as it was. "The problem is that Tory is my mate, so it's not like I can replace her with someone from Feyrion. I didn't plan for this to happen, you know. It just did."

His brother sobered. "All the more reason why you need to meet her like any other Tarradonian male would."

Only he wasn't an ordinary male. He was Fey—one with extraordinary powers. Kenton closed the refrigerator door. He'd lost his appetite. "You're right. I'll teleport to Edendale, cloak myself, and keep a watch out for her. When the timing is right, I'll run into her."

"I didn't mean literally."

That made Kenton smile. "I didn't mean literally either."

Bevon nodded to Kenton's clothes. "You do know she'll be able to see through those white harem pants you wear? The women of Tarradon will find that offensive."

"I always wear this on Feyrion, and trust me, no Fey or Fairy has ever been offended. Come to think of it, I've attracted many a shifter woman wearing this too." It was Bevon who never liked the traditional royal garb. In fact, Bevon hadn't been on Tarradon a month before he'd purchased several pairs of jeans from a store in Edendale, along with a couple of short sleeved and long-sleeved T-shirts. Kenton thought his brother looked ridiculous, but he did blend in better than Kenton did.

He looked down at what he was wearing. "I see nothing wrong with my attire, but if you think it will make Tory uncomfortable, I'll change." With a swipe of his hand, his clothes turned from white to dark blue. He checked again to see that nothing showed. Damn. While his pants were now opaque, the protrusion made it obvious that he was thinking about her. He owned underwear but rarely wore it. He didn't like the restriction.

"You can wear a pair of my jeans," Bevon said with too much

cheer in his voice.

Kenton knew when he was defeated. "Fine. And thank you, I think."

"You know where they are."

If Kenton hadn't wanted to impress Tory, he wouldn't have bothered changing. Once in Bevon's room, Kenton located a pair of jeans and dragged them on. They were heavy and uncomfortable, but he'd deal. His peasant style shirt looked perfectly fine though.

Not particularly pleased with having to adapt, Kenton strode back into the cabin's main area.

His brother looked up and smiled. "You look great, though I suggest you put on shoes."

"I can't please you, can I? Why don't you just tell me to teleport back to Feyrion and forget about Tory?" Not that he ever would.

"You know why. She's your mate."

Kenton blew out a breath. "I'm glad you realize that." He swiped a hand once more and was immediately dressed like everyone else in this realm. "Better?"

He didn't need his brother's permission or acceptance, but it was polite to ask. If Kenton didn't need to see Tory right now, he'd have asked one of his sisters for her opinion on how to dress more mainstream.

Bevon laughed and gave him a thumbs up—a symbol Kenton thought was as dumb as it was odd.

"Perfect. Just don't mess this up, brother. If you do, you'll be impossible to live with, and I'll be forced to move into Fay's place." Bevon wagged a finger. "On second thought, I'd ask Meena to take me in. She's the sweetest of the three."

"Even Meena won't take you. You are too insufferable. Besides, they all live together, you goof."

He grinned. "There is that."

"I HAVE BAD news." Tory's cousin, Detective Anderson Caspian, was addressing the Guardians in their conference room on the fourth floor of the SinCas office building.

Just as Tory Caspian covered her mouth to stifle a yawn, Anderson's announcement had her heart dropping to the pit of her stomach. It wasn't that the Guardians weren't used to gathering at eight in the morning to learn about some current crime spree, but the way Anderson Caspian said it had her body reacting in a not-so-good way.

"What happened?" Tory's Uncle Laird asked, his tone deep with concern.

Most of her family was seated around the twenty-person table—all except the usual suspects, like her brother Ramsey, who never was willing to leave his lab, and her cousin Camden who was just as bad. Naturally, her sister wasn't there since Kaleena and her mate, Finn, were busy having a baby. Tory didn't see her dad and that worried her. Of late, he'd participated less and less in the Guardian meetings.

"We've had four suicides in the last two weeks—all by slitting their own throats." Anderson held up a hand. "I know that's not something we usually deal with, but these deaths are different."

"How so?" Her brother Thane was possibly the most intense member of the group and the one who was always ready to do battle.

"My men have investigated all four cases. As you know, suicide usually occurs in those who are depressed or who have experienced some recent traumatic event. In each of these four cases, the people were successful and happy, at least according to their loved ones. One had just received a scholarship to college, another had been given a big promotion at work, the third had completed his residency at Edendale Medical, and the fourth had retired after a long and successful career in business."

That made no sense. While some rogue shifters had gone on killing sprees over the years, none had been able to make it look like suicide.

"What are you saying?" her uncle asked. "That these weren't

suicides but rather murders?"

"I'm here to ask for your help in figuring out exactly what happened. When we autopsied the bodies, they all had the same unknown chemical in their bloodstream. That hints at a connection between the deceased, even though none of the family members believe they knew each other."

"What type of drug was it?" Thane asked.

"Unfortunately, we can't identify it, which means we don't know where it came from. Even if we did find its origin, we would have to prove someone was responsible for drugging these people right before their deaths. I'm thinking this chemical caused some kind of psychotic break that made them take their life."

Laird whistled. "What can we do?"

Anderson inhaled. "I need your ears to the ground. Talk to anyone who might know if there is a chemical that would trigger suicide."

"Was it a kind of paralytic or a different type of drug?" her brother Declan asked.

"The composition isn't consistent with a paralytic or anything else, which is the scary part."

"I'm wondering if someone slit their throats after they were incapacitated," Declan said.

"From the angle of the cut and the direction of the blood spatter on the victim's hand and arm, the victim did the deed himself. Plus, they all were standing at the time of their death. Before you ask, we don't believe anyone was holding their arm either." He turned to Thane. "I'm thinking Angelique might be able to help."

"Angelique? How?"

"Your mate is from a different realm and has dealt with dark entities. Maybe this unknown substance comes from there."

Greer grabbed Tory's wrist and squeezed hard. Her cousin's mate had been possessed by a dark entity for a short while, and the thought of another one like him roaming around Edendale had Tory's pulse soaring.

"Angelique's realm isn't like ours. It's not like they have buildings where they can manufacture anything. Remember, these entities don't have bodies until they are released," Thane said.

More talking and buzzing erupted, but this time her family settled down quickly. Greer piped up. "Dark entities have escaped before. Could an escapee be inhabiting that person's body for a while and then cut his own throat before exiting?"

Anderson planted his hands on the table and leaned forward. "I actually had considered that, but none of the bodies had any burn marks on them, like they had when you were involved with such a malevolent creature—or rather when your mate was taken over by one."

Tory had arrived dead tired this morning, but the horror of it all had her on full alert now. "Do you have any clues or ideas where we should look?" she asked her cousin.

"None, other than my money is on the perpetrator being from a different realm. As I said, ask around."

Either Anderson was right and the killer was from someplace else, or this person was an expert chemist who had injected the person with some homemade concoction. Though that would be the best-case scenario. The worst would be if it were indeed an entity from another realm. The Guardians were the ultimate fighters, in part because they trained constantly and could cloak themselves when needed. Their particular kind of magic made it difficult for another dragon to attack what they couldn't see. But other world creatures were a whole different story. Tory and her family had learned the hard way how difficult it was to battle even one dark entity. If it hadn't been for Angelique, who was a light entity, Greer would not have a mate.

Tory's uncle looked around. "You are positive suicide wasn't the cause of death?"

"Pretty much, but if we can't find the source of this drug, we might have to tell the family we can't be sure how they died, and that won't bring any closure to them."

"I take it there were no needle marks on the body?" Tory asked.

"None that the coroner found, but I'll ask him to do another sweep." Anderson pushed back his chair and stood. "Thank you for your help."

Camden might be able to figure something out. Greer's brother was a genius when it came to analyzing poisons and unique chemicals. Even though he was a dragon shifter, he preferred to do research rather than go into battle. The sad part, at least to her, was that Camden might be one of the most talented fighters in the group. Her cousin possessed a sixth sense about what his opposition was about to do before he did it.

"Wait a minute," Tory called, remembering what had almost killed her a month ago. Anderson and the rest stopped.

"What is it?" her cousin asked as he turned around.

"What about a dark Fey? Malpan was able to do mind control. He was able to convince about twenty men to work in his mine for free. He was powerful enough to take me out for a while."

Griffin shook his head. "Good thought, but it can't be Malpan, because Kenton Forrester sent him back to his realm where his darkness was removed."

"I know that, but I was thinking there could be other dark Feys here. Didn't your mate mention a man by the name of Balkin who worked for Malpan? He could have been one."

Her brother's brows pinched as he studied her. "She did, but even if this Balkin guy is one, why would he compel strangers to kill themselves? What would be his end game?"

Tory looked around, waiting for someone to come up with an answer, but no one did. "I don't know."

"For the sake of argument," Anderson said, "let's say your theory is correct, and the victims were being told what to do. How would you explain the identical chemical in all of their bodies? Is that something a dark Fey would do?"

Why would he think she'd know? "I have no clue, but we could ask one of the Forresters. Since a few of them are Feys, they should be able to tell us."

Anderson's shoulders seemed to relax. "That's a great idea, Tory. Ask them."

Not her. Griffin should be the one to contact the family. After all, he dealt with them most recently. "I will."

As soon as Anderson left, Greer pushed back her chair, stood, and then clasped Tory's arm before she had a chance to go after Griffin. "Do you really think it's a dark Fey? I have to admit it makes a lot of sense."

"It could be. What bugs me is that these deaths seem so purposeless. I understood why Malpan would want to control his workers, but these victims died. They can't help anyone." Tory brushed some wisps away from her face. "Ugh. This whole thing is sad and creepy at the same time."

"No kidding."

Tory snapped her fingers. "I should have asked Anderson for the chemical composition of this drug."

"What good will that do?"

"Since locating the Forresters is no easy chore, I want to see if Camden can do a deep dive on the structure of the chemical. He might be able to figure out what it's made from and where it was made."

"That's smart, but let's hope it's not made from the killer's own body."

"That is a really scary thought," Tory said.

"No kidding." Greer checked her watch. "Hey, I have to open the store. Do you plan to investigate this mess today?"

"Probably not. I'm too exhausted to be of much good to anyone. I haven't slept in a couple of days worrying about Kaleena. Before Anderson called this gathering, I had planned to visit her in the hospital to make sure she's okay and then take a nap. After that? We'll see how I feel."

"I take it your sister hasn't gone into labor yet?"

"No. There have been two false alarms. Finn and Angelique are with her now. Kaleena's only in the hospital because the doctor is worried about her high blood pressure." To Tory's knowledge, no dragon shifter had ever had that issue. She just hoped Kaleena's dragon was up to the task of delivering this baby.

"She'll be fine." Greer squeezed Tory's hand. "If you need to take tomorrow off so you can be with her, I'll be happy to cover for you."

Greer truly understood what a special twin bond Tory and Kaleena shared. "You are the best. Thank you. I'm hoping she delivers today. I'm so ready to be an aunt."

"You're already an aunt."

Tory's mind was fuzzed from lack of sleep. Chelsea, Declan's mate, had delivered a month ago. "I meant I want to be an aunt again."

Greer placed a hand over hers. "Then go and make sure you are."

After a quick hug, Tory rushed out. Greer stayed behind. She always was the one to volunteer to help clean up the conference room since the Guardians were a rather messy lot when it came to leaving empty coffee cups on the table.

Tory had planned to speak with Griffin about contacting the Forresters, but she wanted to see Kaleena first. Once she exited the building, she had walked about a block when a sharp cramp in her stomach nearly made her knees buckle. It must have come from their twin link. Tory was feeling what Kaleena felt—only on a smaller scale. *Hold on, Kaleena. I'm coming.*

Normally, Tory couldn't communicate telepathically with anyone, but when they each wore their special necklaces, they could. For privacy purposes, she didn't wear it often.

The intensity of that jolt had been more than either of the two before it, implying her twin might even be in labor—for real this time. Because of the quick onslaught of pain, Tory had to stop to catch her breath. While she took several deep breaths, she studied the traffic. Thankfully, it was a Saturday, and the streets weren't very crowded. The hospital was only about a mile away, and Tory believed she could drive there safely, cramp or no cramp. Walking was a possibility, but that would take too long. Her last option was to fly. The problem was that other than landing on the helicopter pad on top of the hospital, there was little space around the building to safely set down. So, drive it was. She retrieved her keys from her purse and headed to her car.

As she neared it, a man with light brown hair pulled back in a ponytail, wearing jeans and a white peasant shirt seemed to have appeared out of thin air right in front of her. Had his body not blocked the sunlight, she might have run into him.

"I'm sorry," Tory said, as she tried to walk around him.

"Are you all right?" he asked, his voice full of sympathy.

Tory stopped. "Yes. I should have watched where I was going. Excuse me, I'm on my way to the hospital to check on my sister." When she tried to stand up straighter, her breath caught again, and her palm automatically went to her stomach.

"Let me help you."

Tory was born and bred to be independent. "I can manage, thank you."

Just then another stabbing pain doubled her over. Without asking permission, the man wrapped his arm around her shoulder. "Where is your car?"

Normally, she would have shrugged out of his grasp, but the waves of warmth that seemed to come from his embrace erased all of her discomfort, allowing her to actually stand upright. That was strange. Or had Kaleena had a short contraction, and it had ended as suddenly as began?

Tory pretended to look around for her vehicle, while trying to decide her next move.

"Miss?"

What the heck. He wasn't a shifter, so how much harm could he cause? "It's the blue car at the end of the block."

"Good. Come on."

Tory could only hope she wasn't making a mistake.

Chapter Two

KENTON SHOULD BE rejoicing that he was finally with Tory, but the pain radiating off her concerned him. "Hand me your keys," he commanded.

The moment the words came out of his mouth, he regretted acting so aggressively, but she was in no shape to be behind the wheel. While a car crash wouldn't kill a dragon shifter, he certainly didn't wish her any harm.

She pressed something that made a chirping sound, and the doors unlocked. Interesting. "Here," Tory said, as she dropped them into his palm.

"Thank you."

Kenton had never attempted to drive before, but how hard could it be? While he tried not to use too much magic while in this realm, now wasn't the time to refrain, especially when Tory's well-being was on the line.

He wasn't irresponsible since he wasn't completely in the dark about how this machine worked. Kenton had scoped out Edendale many times over the last couple of weeks to make sure his mate was okay. During his time of observation, he'd watched many people get into their cars and drive off. He was able to see how fast they drove while he studied the general rules of the road.

Bevon never understood Kenton's lack of interest in this form of transportation, but as far as Kenton was concerned, why learn to drive when he could teleport everywhere? Even Bevon admitted teleporting was a lot faster and safer.

Kenton would be remiss if he didn't mention that during one of his portal-guarding shifts, he'd watched some videos on the manufacturing of cars and how they were propelled. He understood the mechanics. He could do this.

Kenton thought about suggesting to Tory that she let him teleport both of them to the hospital—and then back again—but he didn't want to scare her, especially when she seemed to be going through a difficult time. His goal at the moment was to show her that she could trust him.

Once Tory slid into the right side of the car, Kenton slipped into the left. He searched for the ignition that he'd seen on the videos but found none. Crap. He'd failed within the first ten seconds of trying.

"You've never driven a Sandol before?" He swore she was laughing at him—or rather from the twinkle in her eye, she was thinking about laughing, but then realized it wouldn't have been polite.

Kenton hesitated, wondering if he should bluff or admit his lack of knowledge. After a moment of reflection, he decided honesty was the best path—at least in this case. "No."

"It's not self-driving like many are. Just press this to start the car." She pointed to the button to the right of the steering wheel.

That seemed simple enough. Kenton did as she suggested, and the engine roared to life. Yes! Using his mind, he propelled the car forward, making sure not to crash into anyone. "Where is the hospital?"

She clasped her stomach and sucked in a breath. On instinct, he placed a hand on her thigh. In a flash, her pain disappeared, but if he continued to eliminate her discomfort, she'd catch on that he was not from this world. At least for the moment, he wanted to pretend to be ordinary. From experience, he knew that once he opened himself up to questions, there would be more of them than he was willing to answer.

Tory inhaled and then sighed. "Sorry. Just go straight, and I'll tell you when to turn."

He glanced over at her and smiled. "I'm Kenton Forrester, by the way." She must have heard of his family since so many of her relatives had dealt with his.

She sat up straighter. "You're Fay's brother?"

At least she didn't accuse him of being the one who did things to her body without her knowledge. For now, the less said the better. "Yes."

"Nice to meet you. I was actually thinking about you."

That was news. "Really?"

"Yes. I'd love to chat with you about something, but I have to check up on my sister first. She's having a baby."

"That's fantastic. If you want to get together later, that would be great."

"Perfect. Can you meet tonight by any chance?" Tory asked. "It's kind of urgent."

Tonight? He'd need a moment to think. Kenton did want her to get to know him, and questions were an integral part of dating, right? "Of course."

Tory pointed to the left. "Turn at the entrance."

When he mentally made the car turn, he cut it a little close. The oncoming vehicle was speeding, which normally wouldn't have been a problem, except that Kenton wasn't paying as close attention as he should have. His distraction was because he'd never expected Tory to ask him out.

As he pulled into the hospital parking lot, Kenton pretended to lift his foot off the pedal, even though he hadn't used it once.

"You can park anywhere," she said.

Concentrating, he pulled into a slot and then pressed the ignition button to kill the car engine. Kenton had to admit that driving was a rush. "I hope your sister is okay."

"Thank you. If you want, you can drive the car back to where I was parked, so you don't have to call a cab. Just leave the keys under the mat. I have a spare set."

He planned to teleport back to the eternal flame in the woods. "I'm good. I'll call a cab if I need one."

He pushed open the door and rushed around to Tory's side,

planning on helping her out, but she exited before he had the chance.

She faced him. "Thank you again, and I was serious about to-night. How about meeting me at Wings Bar?"

During his many forays to town, he actually knew where it was located. "Sure. Say eight? For dinner?" Damn. He didn't know if the Tarradonians thought that was too late to eat or not.

She hesitated but then nodded. "Perfect."

The shine in her eyes dimmed as another wave of pain assaulted her. As much as Kenton wanted to help, he thought it best not to interfere. Removing her unease again would create some confusion. "Would you like me to walk you into the lobby?"

She sucked in a deep breath. "Would you?"

He couldn't believe his good luck. "Yes."

This gave him a chance to spend more time with her. Holding her arm, they walked side by side, and he'd never been happier.

TORY'S HEAD WAS swimming. What were the odds that she'd been thinking about Kenton Forrester, and then he shows up just as she was walking out of the building? From what her family had told her, the Feys and Fairies were magical, but she wasn't aware any of them could read minds.

Instead of thinking about what she was going to ask him in regard to the case of the four suicide victims, Tory needed to concentrate on Kaleena. "Thank you again," she said.

"Happy to help. See you tonight."

"Tonight."

At the hospital reception desk, she asked for her sister's room number. With the information in hand, she rushed to the elevators. As Tory neared her sister's room, waves of Kaleena's joy filled her, causing Tory to smile. The door was open, and when she stepped inside the small room, the sight before her made her heart nearly burst.

Kaleena looked up and smiled. "My daughter came a little ahead of schedule."

It seemed like her niece was late rather than early, but there was no need to argue. Tory rushed over to the bed, forcing Finn to step out of the way to make room. Angelique was sitting on the other side, staring at the second addition to the Sinclair family.

"She's beautiful," Tory said.

"Would you like to hold Sapphire?"

Sapphire? Tory loved that name. It was so appropriate considering she might one day run the gem mine. "I'd love to."

Kaleena handed her the adorable bundle who was wrapped in a pink animal blanket wearing a cute, matching pink hat. Her eyes were closed, but her arms and legs were wiggling, almost as if she was trying to figure out where she was. Making sure to keep a steady hold, Tory lifted her up. "She's perfect."

"She is, isn't she? We are beyond happy, though I know I'll be worried about her every second of every day until she learns to fly and defend herself."

The Guardians always worried about their young. They were vulnerable to attack, which was why they had to keep their children's identity a secret. Thank goodness Angelique was there. She would put a protective spell around each Guardian offspring, ensuring they'd be safe.

"How are you really feeling?" Tory asked Kaleena.

"A little bit tired, but my dragon is working extra hard to restore my health."

"I'm so happy for you. Does that mean you'll be going home tomorrow?"

"Actually, once the doctors do a few more tests on Sapphire, we can leave."

Finn dragged over a chair and motioned Tory to take a seat. While she hadn't planned to mention the Forresters, considering Angelique was in the room, it might be a good time to get everyone's opinion. "Are you up to hear about some new drama?" she asked her sister.

Three sets of bright eyes peered back at her. "Always. You can't believe how bored I've been," Kaleena said. "Bed rest sucks. I still don't know why my dragon had to keep my blood pressure up instead of healing me."

"Maybe she was saving herself for the birth."

Her sister shook her head. "I think she was jealous that my focus has been on Sapphire and not on her."

Finn and her doctor had told her she shouldn't shift before the baby was born. That alone would drive her sister crazy—as well as her dragon.

"It's possible. Okay, here is what you all missed this morning." She told them about Anderson's visit and then about what she thought might be happening. "Anderson asked Thane to speak with you, Angelique, to see if maybe a dark entity might have been involved."

She shook her head. "That's not really a dark entity's style. It would leave burn marks, killing the host in the process—unless he was already weak, like he was with Greer's mate. The person wouldn't be alive to kill himself. At least, that is my understanding. Remember, I knew the entities as they existed in my realm—bodiless."

That didn't help much. "It is possible that the dark entity—assuming he escaped from that realm and took over a body—was able to control the victim from the inside. It might have sliced the victim's throat before exiting the body. With the victim dead, maybe there wouldn't be any burn marks."

Angelique nodded. "I guess it's possible."

"Anderson did say there was a strange chemical inside each of the bodies that no one's been able to identify. Have you ever known of a dark entity who left a chemical trail behind?"

"Not that I'm aware of," Angelique said. "Sorry."

"It was worth a shot." Now might be a good time to test out her other theory. "There is someone else who might be able to help.

Kenton Forrester." The looks on all three faces gave her a scare. "What's wrong? I thought he was one of the good guys."

Angelique smiled. "He is. By all means contact him."

For a moment, Tory thought she'd made a terrible error in judgment. "I already did." Tory explained how she was on her way to the hospital and nearly ran into him. "Literally."

Angelique smiled. "Did he say why he was in town?"

"No. I wasn't feeling all that well at the time and didn't think to ask him. He told me his name and then asked if he could drive me to the hospital—or rather insisted he drive me here. He left after he escorted me into the lobby. I was in too much of a hurry to see Kaleena to ask him a lot of questions. Besides, we are meeting tonight at Wings for dinner."

Kaleena reached out and clasped Tory's hand. "That's great, and let me apologize for the pain you had to go through. I was worried that might happen considering our twin link. Just so you know, don't be disappointed if Kenton doesn't answer questions directly. I've heard he and his siblings are rather vague when it comes to giving out information."

"Thanks for the warning. I only want to talk to him about these suicides. If Malpan, who was a dark Fey, could do mind control, maybe another dark Fey is involved. I'm hoping Kenton would know who from his realm is on Tarradon."

Tory studied Angelique's reaction but found none. Just as well. Now that her sister and her newborn niece were happy and healthy, Tory was actually excited to pick the brain of one of the enigmatic Forresters. When the murderer was caught, she would give Wendy, her cousin's mate, an exclusive on the story.

A knock sounded on the door, and a nurse came in. "It's time for Sapphire's check-up."

Tory had forgotten she was holding the adorable sleeping baby. She handed her off and then stood. "Rest, and I'll stop by the condo soon to check on you two."

Kaleena clasped her hand. "Thank you."

"For what?"

Before she could answer, their mother and father rushed in. "Kaleena!" their mother said, seemingly out of breath. Tory was thrilled that their dad looked okay. Maybe he'd missed the meeting because he was hoping for this call.

While she would have enjoyed catching up, this was Kaleena's time. Tory hugged both of her parents and then told them she had a business meeting to attend and had to get ready. Before her mom could grill her, Tory rushed out.

Only when she slipped into her car and it smelled like the faint scent of Kenton's woodsy aroma did her pulse shoot up. *This isn't a date*, she told her dragon.

Uh-huh. When was the last time you met a man and accepted an invitation to dinner in the first ten minutes of meeting him?

He didn't ask me out. I asked to meet with him, and it's for a good cause.

We'll see if you change your tune by the time dinner is over.

Her dragon's smug attitude was quite frustrating.

Tory started the car and headed home to change. Having a Forrester in Edendale would save her a long trip to the forest. It also ensured she'd have a fairly lengthy audience with the esteemed Fey. From the stories her family had told her, the chance of running into a family member at the eternal flame was slim.

Running into Kenton wasn't by chance, her dragon piped up.

What do you mean?

You'll find out.

And here she thought the Forresters were supposed to be the ones who were closed lipped.

Chapter Three

WHEN KENTON TELEPORTED back to his house, Bevon was sitting on the sofa with a beer in his hand. He was watching television and had his feet on the coffee table. What his brother saw in those inane shows, Kenton would never know. Bevon claimed it gave him insight into the Tarradonian mind, but Kenton would rather learn more about how their minds worked in person.

Bevon took a swig of his beer, set the bottle on the coffee table, and swung his feet off the table. "How did it go?"

Kenton lifted his chin in a sign of victory. "We have a dinner date tonight."

All of his brother's mockery disappeared. "I'm impressed. How did you swing that?"

"Tory actually asked *me* out." Kenton was quite pleased she'd wanted to see him.

"Why would she do that?"

"Maybe she could sense that we belong together." Now who was the clueless one?

Bevon picked up his beer and polished it off. "Don't you wish."

Kenton grabbed another beer from the fridge, popped off the top, and chugged a good portion of it. "In all honesty, I believe she needs my help with something. I'm thinking it has to do with those rash of suicides."

"What suicides?"

"Fay didn't mention it to you? Hmm."

"Spill."

As much as Bevon protested, he hated to be left out of anything.

"Fay had a vision, but how or why Tory is involved I don't know. I will find out though. It's what dating is all about."

"Sounds good. What are you going to wear?"

"Seriously?" Bevon was too superficial for his own good. "I'm not changing. I don't want her to think I'm trying to impress her."

"Why not?"

His brother would not stop testing him, though Bevon most likely meant well. "Fine. I'll ask Meena to help me."

"I'm hurt."

Whatever. "You've never dated anyone on Tarradon."

"Neither has Meena."

"But Meena is a woman, and she knows things."

A second later, Kenton landed in her living room. His younger sister had her eyes closed and was sitting cross-legged on her sofa, apparently meditating. He never would understand what Fairies saw in that practice.

Meena smiled while keeping her eyes closed. "Is there something you'd like to share, brother?"

"I need help. I have a date with my mate."

"I figured as much."

"How do you know so much?" He probably would never totally understand his Fairy siblings. "Your eyes are closed."

She finally opened her eyes. "Take a look yourself. You're glowing, and I for one am thrilled for you."

"I am?" Kenton looked down at his chest. Sure as shit, he was lit up from the inside. "How could you tell when your eyes were closed?"

Meena smiled. "You'd think after hundreds of years of being by my side that you'd cease to be impressed by my talents."

"One would think."

Meena slapped her thighs and let out a large breath. "What can I help you with? You seem conflicted."

It was rather uncomfortable discussing with his sister what to wear on a date, but she did have the best fashion sense. "Bevon thinks that for my meeting with Tory later tonight, I should change into something more appropriate, whatever that means."

She laughed. "You look great, though putting on a more mainstream shirt will cause less of a stir. You don't want Tory to be embarrassed being seen with you."

Okay, now he was insulted. "Fine. I'll borrow a shirt from Bevon. Hair down or hair pulled back?" He felt like a girl asking.

He usually pulled it back to keep it out of his face. His decision was totally based on practicality, not on looks.

"Where are you going on your date?"

He didn't want to mislead her. "For our meeting, we'll be at a bar. Tory has questions for me."

"Then pull your hair back, and borrow Bevon's long-sleeve forest green T-shirt. It will complement your eyes."

That was a fairly easy compromise. "Thank you."

"I haven't met her yet, but if she is anything like her other family members, take it slow. When she decides she wants you, you'll know."

"I've taken it slow, and where has it gotten me?" While Bevon was the one who dated a lot—at least on Feyrion—Kenton enjoyed the ladies when the mood struck.

"Considering you have a date with Tory tonight, I'd call that progress."

She had a point. "It is."

Meena crossed her legs again and closed her eyes. "Enjoy each day with her but don't give away too many of our royal secrets. Dating someone who is not a Fey or a Fairy is unorthodox and not without obstacles. But clearly you've made your choice."

"I had no choice. Fate paired us."

"Agreed, which is why you need to take it slow."

While he was next in line to be king, what Meena said did make sense. "Fine. I'll do it your way. Thank you."

"You're welcome."

With a mental nod, he landed back in his living room. "Help

yourself to the shirt," Bevon said.

"Were you listening?"

"No, but I know Meena. She and I both have good taste."

Whatever. Kenton strode into Bevon's room, located the dark green shirt Meena suggested he wear, and put it on. After a quick look in the bathroom mirror, he shook his head at the man staring back at him. While it wasn't his style, he wanted to prove to Tory that he could fit in. He just hoped it worked.

TORY WAS EXCITED about possibly solving this suicide crime spree while at the same time seeing the enigmatic Kenton Forrester. She shouldn't be nervous, but she was. While Griffin and his mate, Danita had recently spoken with Meena Forrester—and she'd provided them with good intel—both had told her she was cryptic at best. Unfortunately, Tory wasn't good with people not coming completely clean with her. To be honest, it pissed her off, but for the sake of the victims' families, she'd try to keep her cool.

Wanting a better explanation about what had gone down when Griffin had met with Kenton's sister, Tory called him. "I'm meeting with Kenton tonight at Wings."

"I'm thrilled you get to have a one-on-one with him in our neck of the woods, so to speak."

"You said Meena's comments were mysterious. You know I'm not good with vague comments, so how do you suggest I handle him? I don't want to mess this up. Too much is riding on it."

"Try to pin him down, but don't alienate him. Our family has relied on his family for knowledge many times."

"I get it. Probe often, but let go when I hit a stone wall," she said.

"Exactly. If he is keeping something from you, it's probably because he wants you to figure things out."

"Don't you worry. I'm very well aware how important this is."

If the Guardians hadn't received help from the Forresters or the Four Sisters of Fate over the years, the Guardians might not have been as successful.

"Have fun tonight."

"Thanks." A knock sounded on her front door. It was Greer, who'd insisted on stopping over after work. She either wanted more details about Sapphire, or she needed to grill Tory about her upcoming meeting with Kenton. When Tory had called her cousin with the news about Kaleena, the topic of Kenton happened to leak out. "Greer is here. I have to go."

"Let me know what you learn."

"I will." She disconnected. "Coming," she called out as she headed down the hallway to the front door.

When she opened it up, a smiling Greer was there to greet her. She rushed inside, spun around, and dragged her gaze up and down Tory's body. "I had to make certain you didn't go all conservative on me for your date with Kenton."

"It's not a date. You heard Anderson. This is me keeping my ear to the ground. Since Angelique wasn't buying the whole dark entity thing, it means there is something else out there."

Greer walked into the kitchen, acting as if she owned the place, and Tory followed. To be honest, they treated each other's homes as their own. "I just visited with Kaleena and Sapphire. I have to say I'm a bit jealous."

Tory chuckled. "She is adorable, isn't she?"

"She is. Makes me want to have a little Guardian of my own."

Tory had considered it, but without a mate, it wasn't an option. "But if you and Blake have a baby, who will help me man the store?" Tory waved her hand to indicate she was only kidding.

"I'd figure something out."

"You're really serious." Tory thought Greer would have wanted to wait since she hadn't been mated for very long.

"Yes. Blake and I have been talking, but we've decided now might not be the best time. His work is very demanding, and we want to spend time together before we add another one to our family."

"I get it."

Greer pulled open the fridge and grabbed a bottled water. Once she was seated at the two-person kitchen table, she drummed her fingers on the bottle. "Moving on to the next topic. Was there an ulterior motive for asking Kenton out?"

Her pulse rose, but Tory was able to channel her inner calm. "No. Why?"

"Did you at least get his phone number? Assuming he has one. I mean he does live in the woods in the middle of nowhere."

Tory laughed. "Are you asking why I asked to meet with him tonight instead of just calling him tomorrow?"

"Yes."

Tory had her answer ready. "The Feys have been an enigma ever since we met them. This might be our one chance to find out who they are and how they know so much. I also wanted to show him the chemical composition of the drug that Anderson gave me."

"You could have scanned it and sent it to him."

Her cousin had an answer for everything. "If I'd gotten his number, I could have, but I didn't. Besides, I wanted to see him. He might have an idea if there are other entities that could be involved in these suicides."

Greer sipped her drink and then placed the bottle on the table. "Tell me what he looks like in case I run into him some day."

That was a fair question. They'd all met Fay at Birk and Lily's wedding, but different relatives had interacted with Meena, Bevon, and Kenton. "He's close to six-feet tall, has broad shoulders, and narrow hips. He pulls his long light brown hair back into a ponytail."

"That is the blandest description I've ever heard you give. What about his eyes? The shape of his face? His scent?"

Her cousin was probing into areas Tory wasn't ready to analyze. "Fine. He's handsome. He has hazel eyes, a heart-shaped face, smells like fresh squeezed lemons, and he has the beginnings of a beard. He kind of looks like a pirate. Better?"

"Marginally."

Tory chuckled. "What?"

"A pirate? Really?"

"Maybe pirate is the wrong word, but he was wearing this loose white cotton shirt that had puffy sleeves. Several gold threads were woven around the neckline. If he'd been wearing leather pants, I might have accused him of being from another era."

"He's probably hundreds of years old." Greer grinned. "You know what?"

"What? Please don't suggest he's my mate." Tory refused to believe that Kenton's touch had distracted her to the point where her pain had disappeared. She'd know if they were mates, right? After all, Tory was a dragon shifter.

"Who mentioned the word mate?" Greer acted all innocent.

Shit. "Maybe I was thinking it, but before you jump to any conclusions, at the time Kenton touched my leg I was having a sympathetic pain response from Kaleena since I was wearing the necklace that joins us."

"And?"

"The pain immediately went away. I just figured Kaleena's contraction had stopped."

Greer twirled the bottle. "What aren't you telling me?"

"It happened more than once. I don't know. He may be full of magic but not necessarily mate material."

"But he's hot?"

"Yes, which is why I want to meet with him in person. I want to see if there is any kind of spark."

"Good." Greer nodded to Tory's casual garb. "Now that is settled, is that what you're wearing tonight?"

"Yes. I dress up for work. I want to relax tonight. I know you love your red pumps, your tight, body hugging clothes, and your perfect makeup, but that's not me."

Greer smiled. "Fair enough, but just so you know, most men

find a well-dressed woman appealing, or so I've been told."

"That's all well and good, but remember I am following up on a lead. And—this is not a date."

Greer laughed. "I can't recall the last time you've protested so much about anything."

Tory lifted her chin. "It's a fact-finding mission only."

"Fine, but there is no law in the universe that says you can't enjoy being with a hot guy."

"I agree."

Her cousin pushed back her chair. "Let's go into your bedroom."

"Why?"

"So you can change. I'm not suggesting you wear a short skirt, a low-cut top, or high heels, but we need to do something with your makeup at least. Your blonde hair makes you look washed out."

Tory grunted. She'd been the subject of many Greer makeovers, and the results were often not to her liking. "I get the final say in this, you know."

"Wait until you see what miracles I can perform."

That was what Tory was afraid of.

Chapter Four

KENTON TELEPORTED TO the rooftop of the Wings Bar and then took the interior staircase down to the main area. He'd arrived early because he didn't want Tory to have to wait. He probably should have asked to pick her up at her place, but then they'd have to either drive her car, or he'd have to teleport with her, and he wasn't ready to spring that on Tory yet.

As he entered the main bar area, the noise was more than he was used to, but if he wanted to have any kind of relationship with her, he needed to get used to it. Kenton snagged an empty table near the back of the room and sat facing the entrance so he could keep his eyes on both the front door, as well as on the back staircase, in case she chose to fly there.

A band was setting up on the far side of the room, and the bar was filled with what looked like wannabe date hopefuls. Definitely not his style.

A waitress sashayed over to him and asked if he wanted something to drink. Kenton smiled. "I'm waiting for my date, thank you. I'll order when she gets here."

The server froze for a moment, acting as if that wasn't cool. "Sure. I'll be back. Just wave if you change your mind, hon." She winked.

Really? She was flirting with him even after he said he had a date. One positive was that at least his shirt and hair style hadn't put her off.

Less than ten minutes later, his body vibrated with a strong energy, and the area around his heart pulsed. Tory was here. Good thing he'd worn a dark shirt so she couldn't detect his glowing light. He was well aware dragon shifters had scales that would shine under certain circumstances, but the average Fey did not. If she understood their connection, he didn't want Tory to think he'd accepted her invitation because he wanted to sleep with her. Okay, he did want to make love with her. In fact, it was never far from his mind, but the timing wasn't right. Perhaps if he'd been more of an expert on the human-shifter psyche, he would have considered it. But since he wasn't, messing up this meeting would cause a shit-ton of problems back in his world.

The front door opened, and his mate walked in. He debated standing and pulling out her chair but then thought better of it. She didn't act as if this was anything other than a question and answer session. For now, he'd let it be.

Kenton tried not to stare, but he failed to keep from admiring everything about her, from her thick blonde wavy hair that lay loosely around her shoulders to her delicately made up face. Her body hugging short-sleeved black shirt that she wore over a pair of white jeans stirred something primal inside him, forcing him to grind his teeth in order to keep from panting. Oh, Royal Goddess, she could alter his insides with a look.

"Tory! How are you feeling?" He thought that was a safe subject.

She pulled out a chair and sat across from him. "I'm good now. Thanks again for driving me to the hospital. I might not have made it otherwise."

She explained how she and her twin sister could feel each other's pain and emotions if they wore their twin-link necklaces.

"You're not wearing a necklace now."

"No. Now that she is out of danger, I don't need to. One time when Kaleena went to Earth, something happened here, and I had to communicate telepathically with her. It worked rather well, but we both agreed it would be a bit invasive for everyday wear."

He chuckled, but it probably sounded forced. Damn. He sucked at this. "I can relate." Not wanting her to ask too many questions about his realm and his abilities right away, he caught the server's attention and called her over. "You want something to drink before dinner?" he asked Tory.

"A glass of your house Chardonnay please," Tory told their server.

"A dark beer for me."

"You got it." The server handed them menus. This time, she didn't flirt. Good.

Kenton turned his attention back to Tory. Keep it professional, he told himself. "You said you had questions for me. We might as well get those out of the way."

She smiled, and Kenton's libido went out of control again. He wanted to teleport to the other side of the table so he could sit next to her, but acting as normal as he could was the only way for Tory to learn to trust him.

"What can you tell me about dark Feys?"

Oh, shit. How much did she remember about her contact with Malpan? Her memory had been erased—at least he believed it had been. Malpan had attacked her and implanted part of his dark soul inside her as a way of preserving his evil nature. If Kenton and a few others hadn't healed her on Feyrion, Tory would have died. Once he'd returned her home, he'd asked Griffin, Kaleena, Greer, and a few others to keep the truth from her. They were to only say that Malpan had merely infected her, and that Greer and Declan had healed her. He hoped no one had said anything.

Right now, he wasn't ready to reveal his part in her healing. That would come later. Having her beholden to him because of that lifesaving bond wasn't what he desired. He wanted her to like him for who he was, not for what he had done for her.

He finally focused on what she'd asked. It was possible she wanted to learn about dark Feys for another reason. Regardless, he needed to answer her. "The dark Feys? They're bad. Did you ever meet Malpan, the man who used mind control on the slaves you helped free?" Kenton had no idea what she remembered.

"Not personally. Danita and my brother told me how he had been able to make people do terrible things. That's why I want to know the extent of a dark Fey's powers."

"What sparked this interest?" Kenton held his breath.

Only when she told him about four recent suicides did he exhale.

"I'm thinking some Fey used mind control on them and made them slit their throats." She locked gazes with him, awaiting his answer.

"It's a good theory, but from my experience, a dark Fey is even more evil than that."

Her eyes widened. "More evil than making someone kill himself?"

He was messing this up. "Dark Feys always have an agenda. What would he gain from their deaths?"

"I've been wondering that too. I've written down what the police detective told us about these victims. I was hoping you could help."

Kenton liked the part about her coming to him for guidance. Tory retrieved a folded piece of paper from her purse and handed it to him. It had the names of the deceased, their age and sex, along with some of their accomplishments. His heart ached for them. They all seemed to be on the brink of something exciting in their life. "Unless the dark Fey wanted that scholarship or the work advancement, I have no idea why he would want them dead. You said the four didn't even know each other?"

"No. The lack of a clear motive is what's troubling me, but that doesn't mean there isn't one."

He liked that she had a keen mind and a desire to help. "I agree." Kenton leaned forward. Even though Tory had excellent hearing, it was loud in there, what with the band warming up and more people coming in. "Why are the police involving you?" As soon as the words were out of his mouth, he realized that might have been a miscalculation on his part. His siblings had mentioned to her family a few times that they knew the Sinclairs and the Caspians were Guardians. *Drat. I need to think before I speak.* "Is it because you are…well, you know…a protector of sorts?" He was certain Tory wouldn't want the name Guardian bandied about in a bar.

"Yes."

"To be clear, you asked to meet with me because you think I might know why someone would harm such happy and successful people?"

Her eyes shone. She'd make a great queen someday.

"Yes, again."

He could work with that. "Any idea who this dark Fey might be?" He kept his voice low, not wanting to announce to the patrons he was aware of the existence of off-world beings.

"No. I thought you might be able to identify those who were dark Feys and those who weren't."

Kenton leaned back and smiled. "I hate to break it to you, but they don't announce their arrival on Tarradon. However, if I run into them, I can sense their evil. My family and I are here in part to keep them from harming your kind. Clearly, we failed with Malpan."

"You aren't the only ones who failed to stop evil from entering the realm." She explained how a Changeling from Earth had managed to get by her cousin Birk by changing his looks. "It took weeks to get rid of that piece of evil."

"I'm glad we have so much in common." Okay, that sounded too much like a pick up line. She was here for answers. "Do you have any other theories?"

"After what you just said, it might not have been a dark Fey."

He hadn't expected her to say that. "If not a dark Fey, then who?"

She explained about the lack of any marks on the body, other than the slice to the throat. "That kind of rules out dark entities who leave burn marks on the skin when they exit. Here's another thing: all four people had a yet-to-be-identified chemical in their body. When a dark Fey enters a person's body, does he leave a bit of himself inside?" She slid another piece of paper across the table. "This is the chemical compound the coroner found."

At first, he thought she was talking about a dark Fey leaving his soul inside a person—not some chemical. When he glanced at the composition, he realized it wasn't a Fey. While he couldn't be positive, he had a good idea who—or rather what—had done this. "They do leave a bit of themselves in a person, but to my knowledge it's not in the form of a chemical."

If it had only been a chemical, he could have cured her easily.

"Then what could it be?"

Discussing something he thought might be true wouldn't be wise. Kenton needed confirmation first. "I can't be sure."

The waitress delivered their drinks. "Have you two decided what you'd like to eat?"

Kenton didn't care what he ordered. He nodded to Tory who picked out a hamburger with fries. "The same," he said.

He'd hoped that Tory was satisfied with his rather open-ended answers, but when she pointed to the paper again, clearly she wasn't.

"Do you know anyone who could find out what kind of chemical this is? I've asked my cousin Camden, but he hasn't gotten back to me yet."

"I certainly can ask. Our family doesn't have any local laboratories we use though." He wasn't about to say he didn't need any since he could use magic.

"I see. By eliminating a dark Fey though, it does help narrow things down. Can you hazard a guess as to what kind of being could inject a chemical into a body without leaving any evidence on the body?"

That he could answer, though it wouldn't be the one she'd be happy with. Kenton lifted his beer and tossed back a goodly amount. The cool brew was just what he needed. "I now have beer in my system, but I daresay there are no outward marks."

Her eyes widened and shook her head. "The beer might be in your stomach, but not in your bloodstream."

"I beg to differ. It's called blood alcohol level for a reason."

"Shit." She looked up at him. "Sorry."

"There's no need to be. You're free to say whatever you want." He thought it cute she believed a swear word would offend him.

She sipped her wine. "I need to speak with my cousin again about where in the body this chemical was found. When he said it had been in the bloodstream, I erroneously concluded that the chemical had been injected."

Kenton was the type to dwell on things too, but it usually just wasted time. "How about we put the death of the four victims away for the next hour and enjoy being here." He waved a hand. "You probably come to this bar often, but I live in the middle of a forest. To me, the energy swirling in this room is a treat. All I get are animal noises."

Her pretty pink mouth opened for a moment. "I am sorry. I was so focused on my problem that I was being inconsiderate. Of course. Tell me what it's like being stuck surrounded by beautiful trees, endless trails, and the sweet smell of the frenlen trees all day."

He laughed. "You do paint a beautiful picture, though I misspoke. I'm not stuck exactly. My family and I are the protectors of the portals between Tarradon and Feyrion. There are several of them around the realm, so we keep busy moving between them."

"Can you go home to Feyrion when you want?" she asked very softly.

"Yes, but it's usually only for official business."

"What kind of official business?"

Kenton could tell this line of questioning would land him in trouble, mostly because telling her too much too soon might put her off. While he had perfected the art of changing the subject, he wanted to be honest with her. She'd be angry enough when she learned he'd kept some vital facts from her. "I'm in charge of the portal guards on the other side." He looked around. Tarradon didn't need to learn about his realm. "I'm thinking this might not be the best place to discuss our protection duties though."

Her face turned a pretty shade of pink. "Of course. I totally understand."

Kenton had the sense that if they had already finished their meal, she would have thanked him and left. He however, wanted to spend as much time as possible with her. "Tell me about your jewelry store. While I've never purchased jewels for a woman, we do have gems and jewelry stores where I'm from."

She smiled. "A jewelry buying virgin! I like it. You have to stop by our store then, and I can show you our fine line of pieces. The Sinclairs and our cousins, the Caspians, are miners. The Caspians mine metals, and we mine gems. We also have a very impressive lab in the SinCas building run by my brother Ramsey. He coordinates the delivery of the materials and checks for quality issues. My cousin Camden is the real genius behind our beautiful settings. Greer and I might come up with the designs for the earrings, necklaces, and such, but Camden has to bring them to life."

He had no idea. "I honestly never gave a thought as to where jewelry came from." Mostly because a swipe of a hand could create many things.

"It's a complex process. Greer and I speak with the clients to learn what they want exactly—or rather what they need. We work hard to make every piece unique for that person."

Her passion thrilled him. "I'd love to see some designs."

As she drank her wine, she kept her gaze on him. "It's a date."

Chapter Five

M OST MEN HAD little interest in jewelry or how it was designed, but Kenton sounded sincerely intrigued. "As I said, stop by any time, but I only work four days a week." She explained how she and Greer split the days, sometimes working alone and at other times together.

"I will stop by in a few days then."

When he leaned back and smiled, something fluttered around her heart. While Tory had no issues dating a human or any kind of shifter, Feys and Fairies were literally out of this world, and she had no experience with them. From the stories her family had told her about Kenton and his siblings, strange things had happened when they'd spent the night in one of the Forrester's cabins—like the whole building disappeared the next day.

She leaned forward. "I agree that this isn't the place to discuss sensitive issues, but can you make things *disappear*?" Tory mouthed the last word.

"If I show you, I'd have to kill you." He winked.

Tory laughed, mostly because she didn't know what else to do. He was kidding right? He must have been, or he wouldn't have winked.

Next topic, Tory. "You have three sisters and one brother, right?" She wanted to confirm some of the things she'd heard. Tory wasn't the type to draw conclusions based on rumor.

"I do."

"Are they all portal bodyguards, so to speak?"

His brows rose. "Bevon and I are assigned to that duty. We're

Feys, and it's our job to make sure only those who are allowed to leave or enter get through. My sisters are all Fairies, and they might struggle to contain someone like Malpan."

"That makes sense. Do you have shifters back home?"

"Absolutely. We're an equal opportunity realm, but we keep out the less desirables from near where I live."

Even she could see Kenton didn't want to discuss anything in detail, especially considering they were at a bar. "Good to know."

"And you?" He asked. "I've met a couple of your siblings, but I'm pretty sure I haven't met all of them."

"I have one sister, Kaleena."

"The one who had a baby."

She'd never said her twin had delivered, but perhaps he'd guessed it. "Yes. And four brothers."

"I bet that must have been hard to compete for your parents' attention."

What an odd thing to say. "Not really. We are all dragon shifters and work for Sinclair mining in one way or another. We all train the same way, too. In short, our family gets along very well." That sounded a bit too sweet, and in all honesty, not totally accurate. "Maybe I should rephrase that. We love each other as a family and would give our life for a sibling, but at times my brothers can be rather infuriating."

Kenton's rather loud guffaw surprised her. "You don't have to tell me about siblings. I live with Bevon, and he is as pig-headed, undisciplined, and irreverent as they come. That being said, I too would give my life for him."

Tory liked that.

The server delivered their food. Since they'd both ordered the same thing, she couldn't get it wrong. "Enjoy," she said. "If you need anything else, don't hesitate to ask."

Kenton unfolded his paper napkin and retrieved the silverware. "I want to get back to something you said. You actually train?"

He didn't have to sound so surprised. "I do."

"What does that entail?"

"Strategy sessions, an obstacle course, mat work, and strength training. It's not something I advertise. It raises too many questions, if you know what I mean."

Kenton waved his fork at her, stabbed a French fry, and ate it. For the next few minutes, they ate in relative silence. Tory didn't remember being so hungry. Perhaps it was because she'd been so worried about Kaleena that she hadn't eaten much in the last few days, and worry tended to burn a lot of calories.

When she was halfway through her meal, she took a break from stuffing her face. "What do you do for fun, Kenton?"

He held up a finger to finish chewing. "That's an excellent question. My brother, Bevon, can watch television for hours, but I don't find those shows interesting."

"You get reception in the woods?" It was possible one of her cousins told her something to that fact, but she couldn't remember.

"We do."

From the small smirk on his face, the reception was accomplished by something other than some focused beam from a satellite. Most of the Tarradon technology came from Earth, but she suspected what carried his signal was something quite different.

"Back to the fun stuff. What interests you?" she asked again.

"I guess everyone's definition differs. I like to read, go for long walks, and watch the stars." He sighed, and she laughed.

"You read that on some dating site, didn't you?"

"Dating site? Whatever are you talking about?" He grinned.

The man was insufferable but adorable at the same time. "Fine. Moving on. Do you hunt for your own food? Since there aren't a lot of supermarkets where you live, you have to do something to eat."

"Distances aren't a big issue for us, but to answer your question, I make my own food."

"You're a chef?" She found that hard to believe.

"Indeed. I see I'll have to show you."

Was he asking her out on a date? If so, she just might have to say yes.

AFTER KENTON PAID for the meal and walked Tory to her car, he watched her drive off. For once, he wasn't ready to go home. Being in this vibrant city actually invigorated him. It was either that or it had been watching his mate enjoy herself. His blood pumped hard through his veins. As much as he had wanted to ask her to dance on the postage stamp size floor, if he held her in his arms, no telling what he might have been tempted to do.

After some deliberation, he decided it would be better to keep this first time more professional. His actions had to be above reproach, and they had been. Now it was time to go back to the forest.

Not wanting someone to become startled by a man disappearing from sight, he found a deserted side alley before teleporting back to his house.

Bevon was eating popcorn and drinking beer while watching TV when Kenton arrived. His brother immediately lowered the volume, dropped his feet to the ground, and sat up. "How did it go?"

Kenton pulled the borrowed credit card from his pants and tossed it on the coffee table in front of his brother. "Great. And thanks for this. I need to get one soon."

"It's easy to do, but keep it until you can get one yourself."

The Forresters had an almost infinite supply of money, but it was Feyrion money, though Tarradon money would be easy to come by. Some of their gems were worth a fortune here. Bevon had actually sold some of them for cash and then opened a bank account. Admittedly, he had to fabricate a few documents like a driver's license, but there was no way around that. No one—other than the Guardians—were aware his world even existed.

While it would be easy to do what his brother did, he had the sense Tory wouldn't see him in a favorable light if he lived off the riches of the royal family. "Thanks. I will, but I'm thinking of getting a job."

Bevon nearly spit out his drink. "A job? You? What could you do?"

"I'm sure more than you. For starters, I'm reliable and a fast learner."

His brother picked up his bottle, tossed back most of the contents, and then waved it. "I'll give you that. Have at it, I say. I take it your date with Tory went well?"

"It did." He gave Bevon the briefest rundown of why she wanted to meet.

"Tory is working on a case that involves four suicides because of some unknown chemical found in the body?"

Kenton nodded. "The problem is that I recognized it."

His brother sobered. "What was it?"

"I believe it came from a demon."

Bevon laughed. "A demon? Here on Tarradon? No way. We would know."

"I thought that at first too, but what else could it be? We can't be so arrogant to believe we know everything. We only patrol our own portals. Who is to say this being didn't come from Cargonia or someplace else?"

"Shit. I hate demons. They are so damned hard to kill."

"Precisely. The last thing I need is for Tory to be asking questions and end up coming face-to-face with one."

Bevon leaned forward. "What's your plan? I'm guessing it involves me."

"Demons will involve everyone. I'll speak with the girls. They are more intuitive than we are. They might be able to sense their location—or rather where they might have been. I'd hate to learn there are several of them here."

"Why would they come to Tarradon?" Bevon asked. "And why kill four people? That would only draw attention to them."

"I agree, but I have no other explanation. Trust me, I want to be wrong more than anything."

"I don't think you are," Bevon said. "We saw that chemical residue a long time ago on Feyrion."

Kenton shook his head to clear it. "Mind control is an ugly thing." Thankfully, the Feys and Fairies were immune, but no one else seemed to be.

"Are you going to tell Tory?"

"Hell no."

Bevon raised a brow. "Why not? If she knows, she can stay clear of them."

Didn't his brother pay attention to anything that had just happened with Malpan? "The Guardians are fierce protectors of their realm. If they didn't realize Malpan was a Fey, they won't be able to identify a demon, yet they'll try to hunt him down."

Bevon held up a hand. "I get it. If they fight a demon, they will die. I wasn't thinking."

"No, you weren't. We tend to forget others are mortal."

Bevon stood, picked up his popcorn bag and bottle, and carried them into the kitchen. "I'll get things started. It's time I visit a few of our old haunts on Feyrion. Someone there will know something."

"I appreciate it. I'll give our sisters a heads up too."

While Bevon went off to ask questions of some of the wisest on Feyrion, Kenton left to ask his sisters for help. Just having a plan made him feel better.

"I'M NOT AWARE of any demons on Tarradon, but then I haven't sensed any unusual unease from any of the Guardians. It's only when I do, that I work to find the cause," Fay said.

"Where are Meena and Tally?" Kenton asked, trying not to yawn since he hadn't slept much last night. Not only did he worry about what the demons were up to, he kept replaying his date with Tory last night. She might have thought she was only on a fact-finding mission, but he bet she had a different opinion once the date was over. Hopefully, she would be willing to go out with him again.

"Meena is off doing who knows what. Tally went back home for a bit. I'm a little concerned about her. I don't think Tarradon suits her."

An in-depth discussion would have to be delayed for another time. They had demons to find and fight. "I agree, but we need her here in case we have to join our magic. Or should I say when the three of you have to join forces." It was the only way to defeat one of these monsters. Correction: cutting off their heads was an option too, but it would take some skill to sneak up on one of them.

"I agree. I'll drop subtle hints for her to return. If she knows she's needed, she'll come back. Tally would never abandon us." Fay's eyes suddenly sparkled. "I forgot to ask. How was your date last night? I heard Meena gave you some wardrobe tips?"

"She did. I wore what she suggested, and while Tory didn't throw herself at me on first sight, she didn't take one look and run either, so I consider that a good thing."

Fay smiled. "Are you going to see her again?"

"She asked that I stop by her store so she could show me the jewelry she designed."

Fay's brows rose. "That sounds promising. I'm glad you didn't alienate her after one date."

"Ha, ha."

Fay got off the couch. "I made something for you last night."

Last night? Meena must have run to Fay as soon as he left. Fay disappeared and returned seconds later holding what looked like two leather wrist bands. "What are they?" he asked.

"This one is for you. It actually has no use other than it makes giving Tory her bracelet a little easier."

"I'm confused."

"You don't own a cell phone, nor do you seem to have any interest in buying one."

Not that he was against technology, but he saw little use for it.

"True."

"If Tory needs you, how will she ever be able to contact you, assuming you haven't mated?"

Drat. He hadn't thought of that. "I plan to get a job near where she works. It wouldn't take much for her to find me."

Fay just stared at him, acting as if he had two heads. "This is a bracelet for Tory. Note, it is made from the same brown leather, but hers has a green Orlandan gem on it."

The Orlandan gem was only mined on Feyrion and had special powers. "It's beautiful, but I don't think we're at a point in our relationship for me to be giving her a present."

Fay smiled. "I see I've been lax in educating you." Before he had the chance to take offense, she rushed on. "It's a communication device. If Tory twists the bracelet around and presses the gem over her heart, she'll be able to communicate telepathically with you. That way, if she is ever in trouble, you can be by her side in seconds."

"Can I track her with this?"

"Yes, but don't abuse the power."

This was amazing. "Why haven't I ever seen this before?"

"It only works when a person has shared his life force with the other person."

Ah. In order to save Tory, Kenton had given her a small piece of his light, which now resided around her heart. It was why they were bonded. At some point he'd tell her, but not yet. "That's great, but how do I communicate with her? Like if I want to ask her out?"

"Place your hand over the band and concentrate. Her wristband will vibrate. The two of you are only linked if the stone is placed near her heart."

"It's kind of like she can call me, but it's harder for me to call her."

"Exactly. Once you mate, your full telepathic link will be complete."

Kenton rubbed a thumb over the smooth stone. "I can't thank you enough. It will give me peace of mind knowing she is safe."

Fay smiled. "That's the point. Now get out of here. I have work to do."

Kenton gave her a quick hug and teleported back to his house. Bevon was already gone, hopefully at work locating the demons.

While his siblings worked their magic on other fronts, Kenton wanted to find a job since he needed to earn money in order to take Tory out. With a little luck, he'd be employed before the day was over.

Chapter Six

WHEN TORY WALKED into the store the next morning, Greer was already there. Her cousin looked up from arranging some jewelry in the case and smiled. "My, my. You are positively glowing. I was hoping you'd call me last night when you got in from your hot date. It must have been something if you were with him for so long." Greer grinned.

Heat raced up Tory's face. "It wasn't a date, though I have to admit, I enjoyed myself."

While no one was in the store, it wasn't really safe to talk due to the massive amount of security cameras that were watching their every move. "I need to check on something in the back room. Maybe you can help me." With raised eyebrows and a glance to the back, Tory signaled for Greer to join her.

Greer leaned closer. "This must be juicy if you don't want our security men to hear," she whispered.

Tory rolled her eyes. Once in the back room, her cousin left the door open just enough to hear the buzzer sound should anyone want to come in and browse.

"It's not that big a deal, but I did learn a lot."

Tory told her about how dark Feys didn't leave a chemical signature.

"If it's not a dark entity or a dark Fey, who else could it be?" Greer asked. "I've never met anyone other than the dark Fey who can do mind control."

"The woman who compelled my sister and Danita could do that. Then again, she turned out to be a dark Fey. I asked Kenton what he thought. I swear he knew something, but he said he wanted to do a bit of research first."

"That's great. Beside all of the Guardian business, how was it?"

Tory had spent last night going over everything. "I'll admit that Kenton does something to my libido. He wore this tight fitting, long-sleeved muscle shirt. And wow. He looked good. I swear when we locked gazes, my heart heated up. It was a rather strange sensation."

"Were your scales flashing?"

"I imagine they were, but I didn't want to look. I'm lucky in that my scales are yellow, so they kind of blend in with my skin."

"Not always."

Crap. She'd have to wear more long-sleeved shirts in that case, as well as keep her hands folded on her lap. "Anyway, over dinner we discussed his family. I have to say, his brother, Bevon, sounds like fun."

"And Kenton isn't?"

"He claims he doesn't really do fun."

Greer smiled. "Then you have your work cut out for you."

Tory laughed. "I wanted to speak with Kenton because I thought he might have information we could use."

Greer lifted an elegant shoulder. "That might have been your original purpose, but the pep in your step, the flush in your cheeks, and the sparkle in your eyes don't lie. You like him."

"I certainly wouldn't mind spending more time with him."

"Good to know. When are you seeing him again?"

Tory couldn't stop the heat from racing up her face. "Kenton seemed very interested in our jewelry making process, so I asked him to stop by for a little tour."

Her cousin winked. "I'll be on the lookout for him."

For sure, Kenton had piqued her interest, but Tory always found enigmatic men intriguing. His full head of hair, the beginnings of a beard, and those intense hazel eyes would make any woman swoon. Add in the fact the man had many hidden abilities, and Tory wanted to know more. Because everyone had vouched for the entire Forrester family, she'd kept an open mind.

Mate, mate, her dragon announced with a great deal of cheer, *and it's about time.*

KENTON WALKED INTO Angelique's Coffee Shop, not liking this feeling of uncertainty swirling in his gut. He was a bit embarrassed that he'd never worked for anyone before, but the son of the King of Feyrion didn't do that kind of labor. On his realm, Kenton was in charge of managing the security for the entire world. That meant he had superior managerial skills, an asset any Tarradonian would want in an employee. He was also a person who was very focused and not easily distracted—another trait any employer would be looking for. Hmm. Maybe finding a job wouldn't be that hard!

"Kenton?" He turned to find Angelique staring at him with her brows pinched.

Oh, drat. Had he been staring off into space? That was not good at all.

"Angelique, how nice to see you."

She moved closer. "What's wrong?"

Being another entity, she could sense things. "Can we speak in private?"

"Certainly. Follow me."

Seeing how both of them were from realms other than this one, she and Kenton had conferred many times. It was nice not needing to hide any of his abilities. Angelique might not be a Fey, but being a light entity was almost as good.

As he followed her to her office, he looked back over his shoulder, glad that the shop wasn't demanding her attention. Once inside, she motioned he take a seat across from her. The space was small and not befitting her talents, but who was he to judge? He lived in the cabin in the woods with his brother, didn't own a car, or have a driver's license. Hell, he didn't even own a credit card. To some, he might not even exist. Kenton wanted to change, in large part to having found his mate.

"How can I help you, Kenton?"

"I need a job."

She barked out a laugh. "Seriously, how can I help you?"

Why did everyone think the idea of him working was ridiculous? That actually pissed him off a bit. "Tory Sinclair is my mate, and I need money to take her out on dates. That's the honest truth."

Her shoulders sagged. "I am so sorry. I really didn't think you were serious. Does Tory know?"

Considering Tory was Angelique's mate's sister, Kenton was certain she knew what happened to Tory after Malpan infected her. "No. We only formally met yesterday."

"Ah, I see." Angelique glanced to the side. "Do you have a particular job in mind?"

"I thought I could pour coffee and deliver the meals to the customers."

Her right brow rose, but she said nothing for a moment. "That seems a little beneath your station in life."

"That may be, but unless you want me to wave my hand and make all of the meals in seconds, that's all I can do. I really don't want to use my Fey skills if I don't have to. I'm sure you of all people can understand."

"I totally get it."

"If Tory and I are to be together, my plan is to...." What was his plan? "Well, when I convince Tory that we belong together, we'll figure it out."

Angelique smiled. "When can you start?"

"READY TO GRAB some lunch?" Greer asked.

Tory finished entering a receipt into the computer. "Almost."

Greer stepped next to her. "You entered all of those?"

Tory faced her and smiled. "I did. It's like I'm Miss Speedy today. I swear my fingers never mistyped a number or keystroke."

Her cousin sighed. "It must be love."

"Seriously? I met the guy one time. Even if he was nice, charming, and…"

"Hot?"

"Yes, and hot, that doesn't mean we are destined for each other." Though Tory had to admit waves of heat would pulse around her heart whenever she thought of Kenton. "Can I ask you something?"

Greer sobered. "Anything."

"When you first met Blake, what did you feel?"

"Loathing."

That wasn't what she wanted to hear. "Seriously. I meant after that monster dark entity left his body."

"Remember, I was locked in a cage, but when I touched him, it was like I had this invisible electric cord attached to my body my whole life, and he'd just plugged it in."

"Did you know instantly he was the one?"

Greer's eyes widened. "I think so, but remember I had been drugged." Greer grabbed her arm. "Hold on. Are you thinking what I'm thinking?"

"No! Definitely not. That would be ridiculous. I mean, he's a Fey, and I'm a dragon shifter." On the other hand, her dragon told her she and Kenton were mates, but was that really the case? Her animal might have just wished it were true.

"But yet…"

Tory let out a sigh. "Okay, okay. When I'm around him, my heart feels kind of funny."

A small smile lifted one side of her mouth. "I'm loving this indecisiveness. That's so not like you. Define this funny feeling."

She didn't want to get into this today. Her head wasn't in the right space, but Greer was too tenacious to let it drop. "Warm and tingly."

"Interesting. How about we discuss this further over lunch?"

She thought her cousin would never ask. "Where do you want to go?" They had about five favorite places.

"How about Angelique's?"

Tory loved the cozy atmosphere and all of the delicious smells. "Perfect. Her coffee shop always calms my nerves."

"That's Angelique's influence not the high-octane caffeine."

"I know."

They locked up the store like they always did at lunch and walked the few blocks to the coffee shop. As soon as Tory stepped inside, a wave of peace washed over her. Without any conscious thought, her hand went to her heart.

"Something wrong?" Greer asked, her gaze zooming to the area Tory was rubbing.

"No. How about we sit near the back?" For some reason, she wasn't in the mood to observe people rushing by on the street.

As she walked to the other side of the shop, she had the distinct sense someone was watching her. Tory whipped around, and Greer almost ran into her. "What's wrong? And don't tell me nothing."

"I think I'm being followed."

Greer looked back over her shoulder. "By whom?"

"I don't know. Maybe my imagination is going crazy. I think those four deaths has me on edge. I wonder if that person who has been doing mind tricks on the victims will come after me."

Greer placed a hand on Tory's arm and led her to the table. "You need a really strong cup of coffee and some food. You're right in thinking your imagination is going crazy."

"I didn't sleep well last night either, which always makes my intuition a bit off." They found a booth and sat down. As soon as she was seated, it was as if all of her worries lifted. "Much better. I think being here is what I needed."

Tory lifted her head to look for a waiter when her cell rang. She pulled it from her purse. "It's Anderson. I wasn't expecting a call from him."

"Answer it," Greer said.

"Hello?"

"It's Anderson. I'm calling to let you know we've had another suicide. This time it was a woman who was a successful lawyer."

Tory's heart dropped to her stomach. "Have you tested for that chemical?"

"A preliminary check indicates the same drug was there."

This was a nightmare. "And so it begins."

"Yes. If you could let your family know, I'll call Griffin and ask him to tell the Caspians."

"I'm at lunch with Greer. I'll let her know."

"Thank you."

She swiped off the phone. "There's been another suicide."

"Well, shit."

Chapter Seven

KENTON WAS IN the café's kitchen picking up an order when his body ignited. Tory was here, he was sure of it. When he lifted a plate with a warmed muffin on it, he almost dropped it. Drat. He'd hoped she'd come in at some point, but now that she was here, he was anything but calm.

He inhaled and drew on his Fey persona. *I got this.*

Pretending he'd been a server for years, he walked out of the kitchen, turned right, and headed into the main room. This muffin went to table number six. Keeping his gaze where he was going, he tried not to look over at Tory. Even though he hadn't spotted her, he could feel her essence pulse toward the back, and the last thing he needed was to drop the plate.

Without a mishap he delivered the muffin, asked if the patron needed anything else, and then turned toward the back. Tory looked up, and he froze. When her eyes went wide, and then a smile spread across her face, it was like watching the sun rise over the water.

Kenton wove his way around the tables until he reached her. He'd met Greer when her mate Blake was searching for her. She might not remember him, but he knew her. "Hi, there," he said, trying to act very Tarradonian.

"Hi. What are you doing here?" Tory asked.

Kenton straightened his shoulders. "I work here now."

"Really? Since when?"

"I just got the job. I'm in training. Angelique said she'd have a uniform for me in a few days."

"That is really cool." Tory nodded to Greer. "This is my cousin,

Greer Caspian. She's Griffin's sister."

"Ah, yes. Blake's mate."

She smiled. "Yes."

There was so much he wanted to ask Tory, but this wasn't the place. "Can I get you ladies anything?" They both ordered a sandwich and coffee. Tory took hers with cream and sugar, though he never would have guessed. He pictured her as a straight up black coffee drinker. "Coming right up."

He spun around and filled out the form for the kitchen. While the cook prepared their sandwiches, he went to work making the coffees. Greer had ordered an Espresso, but he wasn't sure how to make that.

As if Angelique could sense his unease, she seemed to appear next to him. Hell, she probably had just materialized. "Need help?" she asked.

"How do I use this machine?"

"Let me show you."

Kenton watched, but his concentration wasn't at its sharpest. He had the sense that Tory was talking about him to Greer. If not that, Greer was grilling Tory about her response to him. Kenton could see the slight glow around her heart, but most likely no one else could. Was Tory ready to admit she had feelings for him? Or would she keep them bottled up, like a good Guardian should?

"That's all there is to it," Angelique said.

Darn it. He hadn't paid enough attention, but he hoped he could remember enough of the steps to do it right the next time. "Thank you."

"Anything else? Or are you too flustered now that you-know-who is here?"

"Whatever are you talking about, my dear light entity?" He cocked a brow.

"Don't play that game with me, young man. I can out you quicker than you can teleport."

He loved the young man part. "You know I will be eternally

grateful for this job, and don't worry, I will respect your *ancient wisdom*."

Angelique laughed, just as he'd hoped. As soon as she went back to work, he made Tory's coffee. Just as he picked up the cup, however, he forgot what heat could do to skin and immediately let go. The porcelain cup crashed to the ground, sending coffee everywhere. Shit! No other server was close by, but the noise in the restaurant instantly dimmed. Kenton waved a hand to make the coffee disappear, and he reassembled the cup into two pieces. Claire, a fellow server, rounded the corner.

"Are you all right?"

"Yeah. I carelessly knocked the cup off the counter. Thankfully, I hadn't filled it yet."

Claire bent down and picked up both pieces. "I'm surprised it didn't splinter. I dropped one once and was finding slivers for weeks."

Thankfully, Kenton was used to acting calm under dire circumstances. He lifted the broken cup from Claire's hands and dumped it in the trash. "I'll tell Angelique to take it out of my pay."

Claire waved a hand. "She expects a certain loss from newbies."

Kenton smiled. "Good to know."

He quickly turned back to the row of cups, picked up another one, and filled it. This time he was more careful and made it to Tory's table without a mishap. He set the drinks in front of them. "Here you go, ladies."

"I heard a crash," Tory said.

"I knocked a cup off the counter. It's now in the trash."

"Is that so?" she asked.

Did she see what happened or was she teasing him? It was bad enough to be working, but to be clumsy at his job was even worse. "Let me see if your food is up."

Kenton almost teleported to the kitchen before he remembered where he was. Drat. He wasn't sure he was cut out to be ordinary.

"I FOR ONE think he's adorable," Greer said once Kenton headed back to the kitchen. "What are your plans for him?"

"What are you talking about? I have no plans."

"You should ask him out. Go to the movies or something. If he lives in the woods, I bet it would be a treat for him."

"I'm sure he would enjoy it, but why are you pushing me on this?" Greer never pressured her to date.

She lifted her coffee and took a sip. "I like a man who takes initiative."

"Initiative?"

"It's clear he took this job to impress you. I don't think the Forresters need to work."

Tory wanted to understand her cousin's logic. "Why is that?"

"No one else in the family works, and yet they seem to live okay. I'm thinking they have money back on Feyrion."

That did make sense. Even if her cousin knew something, Greer could be rather tight-lipped. "Fine. When he comes to the jewelry store to check out our settings, I'll ask him out."

Greer smiled. "I'll hold you to it."

"In the meantime, I want to figure out who or what is driving these random people to take their lives."

"You always do put obligation before enjoyment," Greer said. Thankfully, her tone didn't hold any judgment.

"It's our way."

"It is. You seem to be very focused on this crime. Let me know if you need me to do anything."

"I will," Tory said.

As soon as they finished eating and then paid, they headed back to the store. Tory went upstairs to speak with Camden. When she stepped inside, she spotted her brother Ramsey. "Is Camden around?" she asked.

"He's in the back room."

It didn't surprise her that Ramsey didn't even ask what she wanted with him. In back, Camden was hunched over a pile of rocks. "Hey there," she said.

He held up a finger, moved a few rocks around, and then looked up. "Hey, cuz. What can I do for you?"

Tory pulled out the piece of paper that contained the chemical compound found in the victim's blood. She explained about the five deaths. "I was wondering if you could see what this chemical is."

"I'd be happy to. Can you give me a clue?"

She explained what she knew, which wasn't much. "The mind-altering, together with the chemical signature, doesn't fit a dark Fey, a dark lighter, or a dark entity."

Camden whistled. "I take it Anderson is at a loss too?"

"Yup."

"I'll check it out when I get home and let you know."

That was all she could hope for. "Thanks."

With that chore taken care of, Tory took the elevator to the first floor. For the rest of the day, she tried to figure out what she would say to Kenton when she spoke to him next. She didn't have his number, so she wasn't sure how to contact him to ask him out. She would have thought he would have at least asked for her number. Or had she been too convincing in making him believe their one dinner together wasn't a date? Darn. Their time together might have started out innocent, but she felt something when she was with him. Could she really be fated to a Fey though? Angelique was a white entity, and she was mated to Tory's older brother, so anything was possible.

Maybe one of the Four Sisters of Fate would know, though she wasn't sure if they would tell her even if they knew. Ugh.

When it came time to close up the store, Tory was a bit disappointed that Kenton hadn't stopped by. It wasn't like he had to leave right after his shift in order to drive home. That would take half a day. Griffin had mentioned that during the Malpan mining tragedy, Kenton was there one second and gone the next, implying he could teleport. Tory needed to make a list of all of the questions she had for the intriguing man.

"You look sad," Greer said.

"I am a little."

Greer cocked a brow. "I think someone is smitten."

"And what if I were?" Tory was a realist though. If they were meant to be together, then it would happen.

"I'd be happy." Greer ran a hand down Tory's shoulder.

Since they both planned to fly home, Tory locked up while Greer headed up the four flights to the roof, since she was still a little skittish riding in the elevator after the dark entity had sabotaged it. Tory wasn't afraid. She took the elevator and waited for Greer to arrive.

"See you in two days," Tory said as they stepped into the fresh air. Greer had the day off tomorrow.

"Let me know if you-know-who stops by," Greer said.

Tory smiled. "Oh, I will."

"Are you going to stop off at Angelique's Coffee Shop tomorrow?" Greer asked.

Tory had thought about that. "I don't think I will. If Kenton is interested, he will make the next move. If he doesn't, then I'll have my answer."

Greer nodded and then shifted. Her cousin lived in a nearby condo whereas Tory had purchased a small home on the edge of town. Once she spotted her place, Tory was tempted to continue flying to give her time to think, but she figured a drink would do wonders for her—or a girl's night out. She wasn't sure if she wanted to sit in Wings though, since the last time she was there was with Kenton. She landed and rushed inside.

"What is wrong with you?" she said out loud to the empty kitchen.

Tory never mooned over a man. Why Kenton? Was it because he was mysterious? She hoped that was all it was.

After she poured a glass of wine, she sat on the sofa, toed off her shoes, and relaxed, debating her next move.

"WHAT'S IT BEEN?" Greer asked. "Three days since you've seen Kenton?"

Tory let her shoulders sag. "You don't need to rub it in. I needed information from a Fey, and he provided it. That was all. Just because I suggested he stop by didn't mean I really thought he would. Kenton was probably just being polite." Damn, but she had believed him.

Greer leaned against the jewelry counter. "If it doesn't bother you at all, why does it look as if you haven't slept?"

Having a super intuitive cousin wasn't helping. "I'm trying to figure out who would have wanted to compel those five people to kill themselves."

"You are such a liar. You want to see him again. Admit it."

While solving the case was important, so was seeing Kenton. "Fine. Kenton intrigues me. After all, he is a Fey." She didn't need to go into detail about how he affected her body.

Greer chuckled, shook her head, and then turned around. Just as Tory went back to work on her necklace design for one of their patrons, the front door buzzer sounded, jump starting her nerves. When she looked up, her hand froze. It was Kenton.

Greer pressed the button. "Lookie who is here," she said in a sing song voice.

"Kenton! Come in." Tory debated walking around the counter, but she liked the safety of having something to rest her hands on.

He looked around and then faced her. "Do you have a moment to show me some of your work?"

"Absolutely." Since Tory understood he wouldn't be buying anything today, she altered her pitch somewhat, showing him the process she went through in creating a design and why she picked those elements.

Kenton asked great questions throughout her small lecture. When she finished, Tory waited to see if he would suggest they share another meal together. When he didn't, she decided to do the asking herself. "There's a good action adventure film showing in town. Would you like to go?"

His eyes widened, and she swore he was trying to figure out a polite way to turn her down. "I've never been to a film before."

"You've never gone to the movie theater?"

"No. I'm on Tarradon to keep the riff-raff from entering your realm, though you don't need to remind me that my family and I have failed a few times."

She shook her head, thankful no other customer was in the store. Tory nodded to the cameras. "That's a shame."

"Aw. I understand. Yes, a movie would be great."

"How about we take in an early show and then do dinner afterward? I like to dissect the plot with someone who's seen it, too."

He smiled, and the area around her heart heated again. She placed her palm over it and rubbed, hoping to quell the pulses. She never had any form of heartburn before, though it seemed to only happen when she was near Kenton.

"Sounds great. I get off work at five. Can I meet you back here?" he asked.

"Perfect."

"I can go home and change if need be," Kenton said.

She wasn't about to ask him to travel across the realm just to put on something else. Besides, she thought he looked good in jeans and an Angelique Coffee Shop shirt. "I'm sure Angelique would appreciate the walking advertisement."

Kenton laughed. The buzzer sounded, signaling another client. "I'll let you go then. I have to be back at work anyway. See you in a few hours."

"See you then."

As soon as Kenton left, Tory's endorphins soared. What was it about that man that made her so happy?

Chapter Eight

A DATE. KENTON Forrester had an actual date with Tory Sinclair! That meant he hadn't alienated her. Yet. She had to know he teleported to work every day, which implied she was fine with that. How she felt about being with someone full of magic was another matter. His goal was to learn to blend in. As soon as he received his first paycheck, he planned to open a bank account. While he didn't have a country identification card, he had no problem creating one. Sometimes magic came in handy.

Kenton walked back to Angelique's with more pep in his step. He had intended to give Tory the communication bracelet, but now he was glad he hadn't. He wanted to have at least one date under his belt before giving it to her. He planned to wear his in the hopes she asked about the small stones adorning the edges. Only her bracelet had the large Orlandan gem in the center.

When he returned to the coffee shop, he instantly sensed something was off. Not spotting Angelique in the main area or behind the counter, he went to her office and knocked.

"Come in."

He pushed open the door and immediately closed it. "Did you feel anything strange in the café?"

"Strange?"

"It could be my imagination, but I had the sense some darkness is here or had been recently."

Her face paled. "Thank you for letting me know. I had no idea anyone else was in town, so to speak. If you wouldn't mind, could you go out there and do a sweep? I'll be out in a minute. We don't need to alert this person that we suspect something. Two magical beings walking in at the same time might set off his radar."

"Sure, though I suspect I might have alerted him already."

He spun around and had pulled open the door to leave when she called to him. "Kenton?"

"Yes?"

"What do you think it is?"

He didn't need to even think. "A demon."

Her hand trembled. "I've never met one."

That didn't bode well. "You're lucky, but if you do sense something, I highly recommend you ignore it. I've only taken out one who managed to sneak through our portals to Feyrion, and it required the magic of all of my siblings to eliminate him."

"I'll keep that in mind, but I'm not without my powers too."

"I know." Kenton had never questioned Angelique about the extent of her abilities.

He didn't want any harm to come to his friend and hoped that if a demon were in the shop he was there to have something to eat and nothing more.

When Kenton headed down the hallway toward the counter though, all darkness was gone. Good. Perhaps the demon had sensed Kenton's presence and left. He better not have come to pick out his next victim.

With a lot of effort, Kenton made it through the rest of his shift. He wanted to believe the world was demon-free, but apparently that wasn't true. Instead of fuming over having a demon in Edendale, he should be focusing on not making too many mistakes tonight on his date.

One plus to his day had been that he made every coffee without breaking anything. He had to admit he'd picked a good job to have. He thoroughly enjoyed chatting with the customers and was even learning the art of flirtation. Angelique had commented that during his shifts, business had picked up in large part to the increase in females—single ones, naturally.

Tory had seemed pleased with his looks, but he understood that different cultures responded differently.

When his shift finished, Kenton debated teleporting back home, showering, and changing, but Tory seemed to take delight in him wearing a work shirt to the movies. Without debating his options further, he walked to the jewelry store. Fresh air—assuming car fumes mingled with the scents of many people counted as fresh—would help clear his head.

To his delight, Tory was waiting outside for him, and his inner glow filled him with joy as did an extra burst of heat. He tried to keep his gait steady since acting too anxious would not look good.

When he reached her, Kenton leaned over and kissed her cheek. He'd seen many customers do that when they met at the café. Tory stiffened for a moment but then smiled.

"Hey there," he said trying to act as casual as possible. "What movie are we seeing?"

"*The Sidwell Adventures.*"

He had no idea what that would be about, but if Tory wanted to see it, he was game. "Are we walking or driving?"

"Driving. It's at least a mile from here, and the movie starts in a half hour."

Kenton was rather pleased when she slid into the driver's side, as it would allow him to study her—his mate and future queen of Feyrion. As soon as he said those words mentally, his heart sank. Tory Sinclair would never want to leave this world—a world where she could be a savior; a world where her family meant everything to her.

Well, damn. That was depressing. When it came time for his parents to step down from their leadership role, he would have to take over their reign. He, too, would have to leave Bevon and his sisters, but since birth, he'd understood his destiny. Why would he think Tory would put him above her family?

TORY WAS EXCITED to show Kenton something new. She could still remember the thrill when her parents had taken her to her first movie. She had been eight.

"Do you go to the movies often?" he asked as soon as the engine fired up.

"Not often enough." Mostly because she didn't have someone to go with. "I realize this is a random question, but do you eat popcorn?"

It was a stupid thing to ask, but she was curious how similar they were—dragon shifter versus Fey. Angelique was from a different realm, and yet she seemed very much like everyone else. Maybe Kenton was too.

"I do."

Yes! "I love buttered popcorn. I also have to buy a box of candy every time I go." She rarely indulged in anything so decadent, but the movies were the one place where eating healthy wasn't an option.

"I look forward to getting some then."

She arrived at the theater in no time. Because Tory had asked him out, she purchased both tickets. It was a bit surprising that he didn't question it, but she had no idea what the dating rituals were where he came from.

Before they went into the theater, Kenton ordered a big tub of popcorn for her and a smaller, unbuttered container for himself. While he asked for a bottle of water for himself, she picked out a soda and a box of candy. When she went to pay, he stayed her hand. "This is on me."

She liked that he was a gentleman. "Thank you."

Inside, the theater was mostly empty, which wasn't surprising considering it was a fairly early show. Only because he wouldn't know which seats were the best, she chose ones in the center.

He looked around. "Where is everyone?"

"Most people take in the later showing." She explained that the movie played over and over again throughout the day.

They didn't get a chance to chat much beforehand because the previews came on, and Tory enjoyed them almost as much as the movies themselves. Every time she looked over at Kenton, he too seemed totally entranced with what was going on, and she couldn't be happier.

For the movie itself, Tory became engrossed in the action and storyline, and it seemed to end almost before it began. The lights came on, and when she looked up at him, she expected Kenton to be grinning. Instead, he looked rather bored—or was it confused? With him it was hard to tell.

"You didn't like the film?" she asked.

"No, I did. It was just a bit confusing."

"Confusing? Which part?" She thought the plot was rather straight forward. She stood and motioned they leave since the staff was rushing in to clean up.

"Why didn't Armand use his magic to get out of his cell? To me, he wasn't much of a hero."

Seriously? "What made you believe he possessed magic? Not everyone on Tarradon has any."

"Interesting. I guess I've been a bit sheltered, but everyone in your family has some."

"True, but we're...well, you know."

"Got it. Clearly, I need some educating." When he smiled, she instantly forgot his comment, though she suspected he wasn't really confused at all. This might be his way of teasing her.

Tory had promised him dinner. Because Kenton had admitted he hadn't visited Edendale very often, she wanted to treat him to a nice place.

A few minutes later, Tory found a parking place in front of the Highlanders Steakhouse. While she hadn't made a reservation, she didn't think it would be very busy at this hour, and sure enough, the place was only half full.

Kenton whistled. "This is where all the people are."

"As opposed to the movie theater?"

"Yes."

He did have a lot to learn. "If we'd arrived two hours later, we would have been lucky to get a table." She studied him to see if he was teasing her again. "You don't interact with a lot of people, do you?"

"Back home? Sure. There might be hundreds gathered for a family dinner, but now I'm used to eating alone or with Bevon, though Meena will cook for the lot of us when the mood strikes."

Tory thought that rather sad. "You need to get out more."

His brows rose. "If I had someone to show me around, I would."

She liked the sound of that. "If you're asking for a tour guide, I'd be happy to show you the ins and outs of Edendale."

"I'd really like that."

The server stopped by their table, and to her delight, Kenton ordered a bottle of wine. Considering the way he rattled off the name of a rather obscure wine, the man must not be the hermit he claimed to be. He looked over at her. "What?"

"How did you learn about wine?"

His mouth opened slightly and then closed. "My home—which shall remain nameless while we are here—has more vineyards than your fine land. Do we have the same strains? Some are the same, but most are native to *my home*."

She was fascinated. "Is the climate different there? Is that why you have so many vineyards?"

"In large part yes. Where I grew up, the weather is always perfect, and it only rains when the plants need it. Otherwise the sun shines."

"It's a magical land then." Tory was pleased with herself for understanding what he was trying to tell her.

"To me it is. It's warm and bright. The colors are more intense, and the plants and ground have a richness to them that I've yet to find anywhere else."

"It sounds wonderful." She wasn't just saying that either.

He smiled. "It truly is."

When he looked off to the side for a moment, it was obvious he missed it. "Why stay here then?"

"It's our lot in life to protect Tarradon and my homeland from intruders."

Now he had her curious. "What kind of intruders?"

Kenton reached across the table and clasped her hand. "Are you sure you want to know?"

His voice had dropped almost an octave. "Yes. It's my job to be a protector."

He blew out a breath. "It's possible that your suicide issue could be a result of a Gromley demon attack."

She laughed, because she thought he was making that up. When his lips thinned, she realized he was serious. "I'm sorry. I thought you were trying to be funny."

"I wish. I don't know much about them other than they come from Cargonia."

She sucked in a breath. "We only have one portal between our two worlds, but I didn't think it had been used for years."

"Apparently, someone has reopened it."

She would have to tell Declan. "What do these Gromley demons look like?"

He glanced around and then leaned closer. "Like everyone else, and that's the problem. I usually can sense their evil, but in order to do so, I have to be close to them."

"How do they leave a chemical inside a person?"

"I've never seen them do that, so I couldn't say, but a long, long time ago, we had a few incidences like it back home. The person always died as a result of their interaction with a Gromley."

She shivered. "How can we stop them?"

"*You* don't—at least I don't think a dragon shifter would have any effect on them. As I said, my knowledge is limited. My family has some abilities, and they've used those abilities to create what I call a magic ball of light."

She whispered with no sound, *a magic ball of light*? "I'd ask what it is made of, but I have the feeling you'd tell me it's composed of light."

He smiled. "You're right."

"What does this ball of light do exactly?"

"If I hit the creature with the ball, it somehow absorbs the demon's energy and kills him instantly."

"You don't think fire or dropping this person from hundreds of feet in the air would do any damage?"

Kenton stared at her for a moment. "I don't know." He held up a finger. "What I do know is that you and your family need to let my family deal with him or them."

Her heart sunk. She shuddered to think these creatures were roaming the realm killing people, and the Guardians had no defense against them. "I will let everyone know, but somehow I have the sense they won't listen."

"I hope for your sake, and everyone's sake, that they do."

Chapter Nine

G OING OUT TO the movies and then having dinner with Tory was like walking on Feyrion where his body renewed itself. After the unpleasant conversation about the Gromley demons was put to rest, they talked about what it was like for her to grow up in Edendale—a town where anything was possible. Kenton would pepper her story with his experiences on Feyrion, leaving out many of the big topics—like how he'd be king someday.

As his tale unfolded, Kenton could sense Tory wasn't ready for his wonderful world of magic yet. The concept of having demons on Tarradon was enough for one day.

After she insisted on paying for their meal, which required him to swallow his pride, they returned to her car. "I would drop you off back at your house," she said, "but unless I fly you home, it would take us many, many hours to drive there."

He smiled. She was so damned cute. "I appreciate the offer, but I have my own mode of transportation. In case you haven't guessed already, I teleport wherever I want to go." He held his breath, awaiting her response.

"I figured," she said with total calm. "I've never actually witnessed anyone doing it. What is it like?"

"I can show you."

She pulled in front of her house and cut the engine. The light from her one-story cottage was enough for him to see her bite down on her lip. "Can we do that later?" she asked.

"Of course." Though he could have demonstrated by teleporting to the back of her house and returning.

Kenton pushed open his door and slipped out. As he walked over to her side to help her, Tory jumped out.

"Would you like to come in for a drink?" she asked.

Kenton's pulse soared, and he grinned at the unexpected request. "I'd love to."

She stopped and then reached out, placing a palm over his heart. "What is that glow under your shirt? I know I can flash a color, but those are my dragon scales acting up. You can't transform into a dragon, can you?"

He moved closer even though something told him not to. "No, not into a dragon. I am not a shifter, but I have my own kind of light inside me." He hoped she'd leave it at that.

"From what?"

Drat. "Let's go inside, and I'll explain it to you." That sounded like a pick-up line, but after sitting next to Tory at the theater and studying her across the table at dinner, it was anything but a come-on. Deep inside, Kenton really needed to touch her, kiss her, and love her in some way right now. It didn't matter that the little voice in his head told him it was too soon. The light he'd put inside her to cure her—his light—had bound them together like nothing ever could, and it was driving him crazy.

Tory stepped past him and opened the front door. "Come in."

He followed her inside. Nice place! Her home was cozy and yet very different from his. Tory's was all light, like some of the homes he'd been in on Feyrion. Even the sofa and pillows were done in pastel colors. The walls had a hint of pale yellow, like the morning sun. While small, it suited his tastes just fine.

Okay, he didn't need to get ahead of himself. If he and Tory mated, they most likely would not live here, and that could be a problem for her.

"I'll get the glasses if you open the bottle of wine," she said with a lot of cheer in her voice. Yes!

"By all means."

It had been eons since he'd been this comfortable around a

woman. Once the females on Feyrion understood who he was, they treated him like some prize to be won. He shivered at the remembrance of all the terrible dates he'd had to endure. It took forever to convince his parents that he wanted to wait until he found his one and only true mate.

"Are you okay?" she asked.

Surely, she couldn't have sensed the dismay in him, or could she? "I'm good."

Tory smiled and then handed him the bottle and the opener. "Use your magic on this."

Kenton wouldn't use magic. He'd open it the old-fashioned way. As soon as she placed the glasses on the counter, he popped the cork and poured the wine.

Kenton lifted his glass. "To a great evening, for the movie, the dinner, and for showing me your delightful city. I didn't realize how closed off I've been living in the forest."

Tory sipped her drink and then stepped closer to him. With her so near, his eyes had to be flashing gold by now. For sure his life light was going crazy—as was hers. He doubted she'd even noticed the light pulsing around her heart though, because a lot of yellow was glowing under her skin.

"Are you a yellow scaled dragon?" he asked, needing to say something other than demanding she kiss him.

Tory glanced down at her arms. "I'm a black dragon with some yellow scales interspersed. I realize that most dragons around here are all black, but the Guardians have an added color. We've always been led to believe it was the magic imbued in us."

"Magic, huh?"

She lifted a shoulder. "Nothing really fancy."

"What can you do?" He'd show her some of his abilities if she showed him hers.

"We can become invisible while in our dragon form." Tory lifted her chin. He was thrilled she was proud of her talents.

"Can you do this?" Kenton cloaked himself, and her eyes went wide. Two seconds later, he reappeared.

"Oh, my goddess. Can you do that whenever you want?"

His libido skyrocketed. "Yes."

"That's incredible."

Kenton wouldn't tell her that was how he knew when to run into her when she was on her way to the hospital to visit her sister. He'd been watching her from across the street from SinCas for a while.

"I have a few other tricks, but if I keep them secret a bit longer, I might be able to convince you to go out with me again." He could almost see his brother roll his eyes at that line.

"Sounds good to me." Tory set down her glass. "Now that we have that out of the way, do you want to explain why your chest is glowing?"

Just as he was about to tell her, she unbuttoned a few of his shirt buttons and then peeked under the material. At that moment, he thought his heart would burst. He set down his glass and gently clasped her wrist. "That is dangerous territory, young lady."

She laughed. "Why is that?"

"My heart glows only when I am with someone very special to me." Thank goodness, he didn't tell her the whole truth—that she was his mate.

Tory retracted her hand, but her eyes flashed the most beautiful shade of purple. She shoved up her sleeves to expose delicate yellow translucent scales under her skin that were blinking up a storm. "I do this when I'm with someone I find attractive."

Blood pounded in his ears, forcing him to control himself. He feared he'd ravish her right on the kitchen counter. "Want to do a little experiment?"

The pulse at the base of his neck throbbed hard.

"What kind of experiment?" she asked in the flirtiest tone he'd ever heard.

"This."

Kenton pulled her close and kissed her hard, with all of the passion that was flowing through his body. The heat around his heart nearly seared him, but he guessed it was the same for her. They belonged to each other, and he would tell her just as soon as they were truly together.

TORY WAS OVERWHELMED with need and desire. She never thought she'd be kissing Kenton Forrester in her kitchen tonight, but the moment they toasted, she was drawn to him like two magnets of opposite polarity. Her scales pulsed to the same tempo as the glow around his heart.

Somehow her hands found their way around his neck, and she leaned in closer. When he begged for entrance, Tory didn't think twice. Without breaking their seal, he spun her around so that her back was against the kitchen counter. The tongue-twisting exploration did things to her insides that she'd never felt before. It was as if they were connecting on an elemental level, and she wasn't convinced she'd be able to stop anytime soon.

Kenton cupped her face and groaned. If his eyes hadn't turned the most amazing gold color, she wouldn't have leaned back. "Your eyes! They are gorgeous."

"Not any more gorgeous than your purple ones."

There were so many things she wanted to ask him. Everything about Kenton seemed so normal and yet so different. When she dragged her hand down over his shoulder and placed her palm on his heart, her skin nearly singed. "Does it hurt?"

"Not when I'm with you."

From the way his eyes were hooded, looking at her with such longing, she had to move closer. She then slipped her hands under his green T-shirt and lifted it out of his jeans.

Kenton stepped back. "Time for another one of my talents." With a swipe of his hand his shirt disappeared.

She giggled. "Where did it go?" He nodded to the neatly folded shirt on the counter. "How is that possible?"

He grinned and then dragged a knuckle down her cheek. "I'm a Fey. I'm full of magic."

This was amazing. "Can you do that to my shirt?"

When a cool breeze shot across her chest, she looked down. Her shirt was gone, but not her bra.

"Want me to keep going?" he asked with a devilish grin.

"How about a few more kisses first?" she asked as she toed off her shoes.

"I'll never turn down a kiss from a beautiful blonde."

If that was a line, she didn't care. She pretended he meant it. Tory probably should have suggested they move to a more comfortable place, but this make-out location was almost forbidden and therefore more exciting. Not only that, she didn't want to spoil the mood by suggesting they move.

Tory threaded her arms around Kenton's waist, tilted her head back, and when his lips met hers, she moaned. His kiss was soft yet demanding, strong but giving. Out of the corner of her eye, the light show she was providing bounced off the kitchen walls. Oh, my. Never had she been this turned on before.

His hands slid from her waist upward, and when his thumbs brushed over her bra, she wanted nothing more than for him to touch her intimately. She let go of him and reached around her back. Before she could unhook the clasp, her bra disappeared.

"What just—?"

Kenton leaned back and smiled. "Like I said. I'm a man of many talents."

"I'm not sure I'll get used to this. Can you magically create a condom?" Holy shit. Did she just say that?

He snapped his fingers, and one appeared in his hand. Her pulse shot skyward. This was almost too much to absorb: disappearing clothes, teleporting, creating objects out of thin air.

Before she could ponder his extensive abilities, his magic tongue nabbed a nipple while his hand cupped her free breast. He flicked,

licked, and tugged all the while kneading her other breast, occasionally plucking her nipple between his thumb and forefinger. The more he licked, the faster his fingers moved. Despite his apparent desperation, Kenton remained gentle.

Needing more tactile stimulation, she dug her nails into his shoulders. Just as the pressure Kenton was exerting on her body was about to push her over that first climactic edge, Kenton stopped and lifted her onto the counter.

He straightened and then smiled. "Your skirt has to go."

"I give you permission to zap it off," Tory said, not remembering the last time she'd been so forward with someone she barely knew. The thing was though, it felt as if they had met in another life, which was clearly impossible.

Instead of the expected wave of a hand, Kenton unzipped the back of her skirt like a normal human would. She lifted up a bit, and he tugged the material down her hips, taking her panties with it. He whistled. "You are more beautiful than in my dreams."

His dreams? Sure, he'd entered her dreams once or twice—okay, every night—but she didn't think it was the same for him. But maybe it was. When he widened her legs and bent over, Tory instinctively slid forward and then dropped back onto her elbows. A second before her skin hit the counter, his folded shirt magically appeared under her. Whoa! Just breathe, she told herself.

Tory half expected to wake up and find this was all a dream, but from the way her body was exploding with need, this was completely real.

The first swipe of his tongue between her legs had her sucking in a deep breath. It was as if he'd set every nerve ending on fire with that one lick. She closed her eyes and let the wonder of it all sink into her. The area around her heart heated, her teeth elongated, and her nails sharpened. To say she was excited would be an understatement.

While Kenton didn't seem to need any encouragement, she panted and groaned, wanting him to take more. "Yes. Don't stop."

And he didn't. The onslaught of erotic elation kept coming in waves until her orgasm arrived hard and fast. Chest heaving, she dropped back onto the counter.

Kenton stopped. "I see you liked that."

"Funny man," she managed to say.

The tearing of the condom sounded louder than it should have, and she sat up. "I wanted to return the favor."

"Next time, my love." In a flash, he pulled her onto her feet and spun her around. "As much as I want to kiss you for the next hour, I can no longer hold out."

She couldn't either. Tory planted her hands on the counter and spread her legs. When he cupped her already sensitive breasts, more lust coursed through her. He pressed his chest against her back and swept her hair out of the way, exposing her neck. Because he wasn't a shifter, she didn't think he planned to bite her.

Instead, he kissed his way from her shoulder blade up her neck to her sensitive earlobe. "I love doing this," he whispered as he pressed on her nipples and placed his large cock against her opening.

She lowered her head to give him more access. *I love you doing this to me.* Good thing they couldn't communicate telepathically since some things were better left unsaid.

Using his hands to distract her or possibly just to drive her insane, he slid his cock into her. Because of his large size, it reached only halfway, however Kenton didn't seem bothered by the restriction. He slowly eased out and nudged his way back in again. This time he filled her completely. Her stomach contracted, and her breath whooshed out of her. If she didn't know it was impossible, she would have said he had filled her with his light.

He stayed deep in her for a few seconds before retreating again. He then lowered his hands to her waist and held her still while he thrust into her again and again. Each time, her body lit up more, causing her second climax to build.

His lips found the crook between her neck and shoulder blade and then gently dragged his teeth across the surface. While he was distracting her with his talented tongue, he withdrew his cock and stayed half in and half out for what seemed like forever. Not one to be timid, Tory slammed her hips backward, taking him deep into her again.

"That did it," he mumbled.

For the next few seconds they both pulled and pushed until she came harder than she ever had, and Kenton exploded seconds later. Only after his pulsing stopped did he press his cheek against the back of her head and wrap his arms around her.

Neither said anything for a while. Tory at least, was trying to come to grips with what just happened. It was almost surreal.

Kenton eventually withdrew, placed his hands on her shoulders, and lifted her up. He then turned her around. "I have no words."

"Neither do I."

He stepped back, swiped a hand, and was instantly dressed. While she didn't want to put on her work outfit, she was a little self-conscious about being totally naked. "Let me grab a robe. Be right back."

As she trotted down the hallway, his fingers still seemed to burn on her skin. What had she just done? She'd slept with some magical Fey is what. Where was the future in that? Kenton Forrester had charmed her, plain and simple. She wondered if his innocent act had been a ruse to get her into bed—or rather into her agreeing to have sex with him. Or was she overthinking it all?

By the time she donned a pair of panties, threw on a robe and returned, she'd decided this might have been the biggest mistake of her life.

There was one problem.

Kenton wasn't there to tell him.

Chapter Ten

"YOU JUST LEFT after sex?" Bevon asked. "Without saying goodbye?"

"Don't hassle me. I feel guilty enough. I could sense she was having regrets and thought it best if I leave."

"What the fuck is wrong with you, bro?"

"I didn't want to overstay my welcome. I thought it would embarrass her if she had to tell me to bugger off."

Bevon shook his head. "You're a dick, and I'll leave it at that. Did you at least give her the communication bracelet that Meena made?"

"Not yet. It was too soon."

"Too soon? You had sex with her. What are you waiting for?"

Kenton hadn't been thinking straight. "I will when the time is right."

"I can see I can't talk any sense into you. I'm out of here." His brother disappeared.

"Fine," Kenton said to an empty room.

Bevon claimed his favorite spot at night was on top of some mountain overlooking the sea, saying it was where he went to think. Maybe Kenton should go to his peaceful place. It was in the middle of a frenlen forest where the needles cushioned the ground. Next to his spot was a small but fast-moving stream. That area brought him peace—something he could use right now.

His other option was to talk to Meena. If it hadn't been so late, he would have. Though knowing her, she'd tell him to go back to Tory and apologize. Heading back to Feyrion wasn't a viable option either as that would be admitting he was wrong. It was always possible his life light was just in need of renewal. The lack of power might have messed with his ability to think clearly.

For now, the best solution was teleporting to his place of peace. Once there, he sat cross-legged in the middle of a small clearing that was surrounded by trees. Kenton looked up and studied the stars. While he continued to second-guess his decision to leave Tory, he finally decided on his next step. He'd give her a few days to settle down, and then he'd apologize. In the meantime, he planned to keep a very close eye on her. Staying invisible took a lot of energy, but he could handle it for short periods. Had he not given her part of his life light, he'd have had a bit more strength.

From past experience, he understood that overanalyzing a situation led to poor choices, so he stretched out and inhaled the freshness of the frenlen and told himself tomorrow would bring more clarity.

"KENTON SENT YOU flowers?" Greer asked at the store the next day. "That must have been one hell of a movie you went to."

"Funny, funny." Tory wasn't in the best of moods. What did his gift mean exactly? That he was sorry for literally disappearing on her? Or was he asking for another date? "Fine. If you must know, the sex was mindboggling and amazing. It was better than anything I'd ever experienced. It was—"

"I get it. You liked it, and I'm guessing Kenton did too."

"Yes. Or so I thought. After we ah…finished…I needed to change since we were in the kitchen naked and all."

"The kitchen?"

"Don't judge. We happened to be in there when the kissing started. Anyway, afterward I went into the bedroom to grab a robe. In the time it took to throw something on and return, he'd left."

"I thought you said you drove."

"I did, but Feys can teleport—or at least Kenton can."

Greer's eyes widened. "Like the Four Sisters?"

"Yes, just like them."

"Wow. Why do *you* think he left?"

Tory hadn't slept much last night trying to figure that out. "I don't know. It wasn't like I took a lot of time changing. Sure, I asked myself what had just happened, but I don't think he can read minds."

Greer tilted her head. "Maybe he can. You said he was magic. Remember when Blake and I visited the eternal flame?" Tory nodded. "Meena seemed to know what I wanted before I said a word."

That was a scary thought.

"Meena also knew who I was before I said anything," Greer said.

"Okay, maybe he was giving me some room to come to grips with what this might mean." She thought about that for a few seconds. "But why leave? It wasn't like I was regretting what we'd done. As I said, it was epic."

"I sense a *but* coming. What were you feeling exactly?"

Tory blew out a breath. "Maybe I was feeling a little insecure knowing that someone as powerful as Kenton would want to be with someone like me."

Greer grabbed her arm. "Are you crazy? You're a freaking Guardian. We have our own magic. Can he fly?"

"No. He's not a shifter."

"That's one thing you have on him."

Greer had a point. "Fine. Do you think the flowers are a way of saying he's sorry for ditching me?"

Greer's brows pinched. "Why, Tory Sinclair, I believe you really like him. You've never doubted yourself in the past. Why now?"

"I don't know. That's why I'm so confused."

"Look, I say accept his apology and go out with him again. Ask Kenton straight out why he left. He might have thought he shouldn't have taken advantage of you."

"He didn't take advantage of me. Trust me, I was more than

willing. If anything, I almost seduced him. I unbuttoned his shirt first."

Greer chuckled. "Then all will be well. Trust me." Her cousin leaned back against the counter. "I say we have lunch at the coffee shop today. If Kenton is there, you can act as if his leaving didn't bother you one bit."

She liked that idea. "You're right. Men don't like women who are easily upset. He might have had a good reason for leaving."

"Exactly."

Tory checked her watch. "Since no one is here and lunch isn't for another hour, I want to check with Camden to see what he learned from that chemical signature found inside the dead bodies. Kenton seems to think it was from some kind of demon, and I want to find out if Camden can corroborate that theory."

"You go. I'll hold down the fort." Greer leaned in and hugged her.

"Thanks."

Once upstairs, Tory stepped into the lab where both her brother Ramsey, as well as Camden, were busily working. "Hello, boys."

They both looked up. Ramsey was seated at his computer doing something that involved business most likely, while Camden was filing a piece of metal. He slipped off his goggles. "I was about to come see you."

A rush of hope shot through her. "What did you find?"

"I'm not sure. The compound you gave me was a mix of human DNA as well as something foreign."

"Not anything man made then?"

"No. It was almost as if this thing got inside the person—like that dark entity was able to do to Blake. Once inside, it might have commanded the person to kill himself. After the host died, it left."

That was a bit far-fetched, but it wasn't out of the question. "I was talking with Kenton yesterday, and he thought it might be a kind of demon."

"You spoke with the Fey, Kenton Forrester?"

She didn't know why her cousin sounded so surprised. "Yes. I had a date with him. He seemed to recognize the chemical, though he said nothing about this demon possessing a person like that."

"Next time you see him, ask if this demon can enter and exit a person without a trace."

"I will and thank you for doing all this extra work."

"Any time."

"To be clear, you are saying that it could have been a demon?" she asked.

He shrugged. "I know nothing about them, but I wouldn't rule it out. As I said, ask Kenton."

"I will. Thank you. Would you mind sending your findings to Anderson?"

Camden smiled. "I already did. I also sent it to both of our fathers so the entire Guardian community will know."

"You are the best." She smiled, spun around, and left.

"What did Camden say?" Greer asked the moment Tory stepped into the shop.

Tory couldn't blame her eagerness for finding the truth. All of the Guardians were on edge. With five very similar deaths and no end in sight, everyone was working hard to find this person—or this thing. "Nothing really conclusive."

She explained what Camden had figured out.

"What's next?" Greer asked.

"I don't know. If we assume it is a Gromley demon like Kenton believes, this thing is dangerous. I get the sense it has an agenda, only I have no idea what that could be."

"I would pick Kenton's brain some more."

"I plan to, but when we first discussed it, he didn't seem to know much about them other than they were from the Cargonia realm," Tory said.

"Cargonia? Other than taking a little trip to Earth and speaking with Zane Barrows—the hunky werebear who hails from there—we should try the Four Sisters. They might know something."

"They are the Four Sisters of *Fate* for a reason. They help mates. Why would they know anything about demons?"

"Just saying. They are special. I wouldn't put it past them to at least be aware of these Gromley demons."

"It's worth a shot. After we close, maybe we should take a trip to their shop."

Greer pressed her lips together. "Blake and I have something planned for tonight. Do you think you could go alone or maybe ask Kenton to join you?"

"Sure." Though she had no way of getting a hold of the man. He really needed to embrace the modern times.

WHEN TORY AND Greer stopped over at Angelique's Coffee Shop for lunch, it happened to be Kenton's day off, which put Tory in a bad mood for the rest of the day. She should have been happy not to have to run into him, but she had wanted to know what he knew about these demons.

Okay, okay. She wanted him to apologize or at least explain his strange behavior last night, but now she'd have to wait. He only lived an hour's flight away, but none of her siblings had ever spotted any permanent homes nearby, so it might be a waste of time if she went there. If she could be sure they would be dating in the future, she'd buy him a stupid phone and even pay for the monthly service charge. Even if he couldn't use the phone while in the forest, he could teleport to town and call her. Grr. He was so frustrating.

When five o'clock rolled around, Greer said she'd close up and told Tory to head on over to the Four Sisters Pottery Shop. They both understood how important it was to learn about these demons.

Once Tory landed in front of their shop, she shifted and went inside. Magnolia and Acacia were manning the store. Tory admired both women. They'd just had babies, yet no one would have been able to tell from their trim figures.

Magnolia was checking someone out, so Acacia came over to her. "Tory, this is a pleasant surprise."

"Thank you." She looked around. "Could we speak in private?"

"Of course. Follow me." Acacia looked over at her sister and nodded.

Apparently, all of the sisters had the ability to communicate telepathically with each other. What Tory wouldn't give to be able to do that with her family.

Acacia showed her into the kiln room in back. While it was rather warm in there, being surrounded by shelves full of glazed and unglazed works of art was cozy and comforting. Acacia motioned they sit at the four-seater table.

"Tell me what troubles you."

Tory was almost surprised Acacia didn't already know. "There have been five nearly identical suicides recently."

"I've read about that. They were tragic and meaningless."

"Yes, they were. We have some evidence that points to someone having helped these people slit their throats."

Acacia's brows rose. "Do you know this person's identity?"

Tory explained what Kenton had said. She noted that as soon as she mentioned the Fey's name, Acacia seemed to focus on every word. It was almost as if she respected his opinion a lot. "Do you know anything about these Gromley demons?" Tory asked.

She pressed her lips together. "Yes and no. If I recall, there was a group of them who lived on Tarradon quite a long time ago."

"I thought they were from the realm of Cargonia."

"Now they are, but how or why they moved, I couldn't say."

"Do you have any idea how to chase them off? Or kill them should the need arise?"

A quirky smile lifted Acacia's lips. "What does Kenton say?"

That was odd. Acacia must be convinced he was the key. Either he'd been lying to her about what he knew, or he really didn't know—other than if he threw some magical ball at the guy that it would kill him. "He used some magic against them in the past, but that won't help the Guardians who are out hunting this person."

She shook her head. "I would ask your family to back off for now." She tapped a slightly clay encrusted nail on the table. "I might be able to help, but I'll need time. Can I call you when I know more?"

No Guardian had ever turned down an offer from a powerful sister. "Of course."

Tory was about to write down her number when Acacia slightly shook her head. "I know it."

Tory wouldn't ask how. "Thank you for your help."

"Of course. I'll be in touch."

Chapter Eleven

TORY WAS NERVOUS. She'd not met the amazing Ophelia, grandmother to the Four Sisters of Fate, but she'd heard stories from both Finn and Chelsea McKinnon about her. They'd both grown up in the town of Silver Lake, Tennessee where Ophelia now resided.

Tory swore every Guardian was crowded around the conference table, including her dad, who wasn't looking particularly well. Now wasn't the time to question him about his health, however. Even if she did, he'd just tell her he was fine. It was the Sinclair way.

What concerned her the most was that dragon shifters didn't get sick, unless it was by the hand of someone evil. When she'd asked her mom about it, she said that Jamison hadn't been in a fight or anything, and that all he needed was a little rest. Tory wasn't buying it. He wasn't that old.

Camden and Ramsey rushed in. Tory had asked her cousins to be there since Camden analyzed the chemical residue, and Ramsey worked with him, but to be honest, she almost expected them to blow her off. She couldn't remember the last time either of them had been to a meeting of the minds.

Due to the lack of seats at the main conference table, they had to sit in a row of chairs placed along the wall.

Uncle Laird stood. "I know it is late. I appreciate you all dropping everything at such short notice, but Ophelia's time here is short. We very much appreciate her coming from Earth. Without further ado, I'll hand the floor over to her. Ms. Ophelia, if you will?"

She smiled, and she almost looked youthful for a moment. Everyone who'd met the ancient witch claimed she was over ninety, but looks were often deceiving.

"Some of you might not know that I came from Tarradon originally and that I lived here for many years. That was a long time ago, but those days were wonderful. It was where I met my mate and where I had my wonderful children." She held up a hand. "But I digress. I won't admit whether I was living here four hundred years ago or not, but I do know my history. The Gromleys were a strange lot." She inhaled and glanced around as if to let everyone absorb this news.

"Strange how?" Declan asked.

"Whenever they became irate, their appearance changed. I wouldn't call them shifters, but their body would transform into something that looked like glowing embers, though not as bright. It's hard to explain. Back then, there were few people on Tarradon, so no one could explain this odd reaction to a change in emotion. It's not surprising that most who witnessed this transformation were afraid of them. The other locals made up stories to explain this bizarre and unique behavior—from them being devils to being dark witches."

"That's similar to what happened to some of the women who lived in Salem—a small town in the United States. They were labeled as witches and burned to death," Finn said. "While I wasn't alive back then, I'm not proud of the way we treated our people."

Ophelia nodded. "I'm glad you understand. As you can imagine, these Gromleys were persecuted. What was misunderstood was feared."

"How did they end up on Cargonia?" Tory asked.

Ophelia sighed. "That's the sad part. I don't recall the details, but apparently the locals decided that the only way to get rid of these pests was to slaughter them. Back then, a simple throat cut would kill them."

The irony wasn't lost on her. "But they didn't all die."

"No. Many did though. The rest fought back. Again, I don't know what happened exactly, but a group of white lighters banded together and did a spell to cast them out."

A spell that clearly worked. Until now. "I know four hundred years is a long time, but do you think they are back for revenge?" Tory asked.

"That I couldn't say. You'll have to ask them."

"Do you know if these demons are able to inhabit a person's body?" Anderson asked.

All heads swiveled from the detective back to Ophelia.

"Are you asking if they are similar to a dark entity?" He nodded. "Not that I know of. I'm sorry."

"I think that is enough questions for her," Acacia said. "She tires easily."

Tory didn't get that sense, but maybe Ophelia had telepathed to her granddaughter that she had told them all they needed to know.

Ophelia pushed back her chair, and Acacia was there to help her up. Uncle Laird stood and rushed over to help the old lady as well. "You've been a huge help," he told her.

"I wish I knew more."

As soon as Acacia and Ophelia left, the room erupted in chatter. Anderson rapped a knuckle on the table a minute later. "We all need to think about this new development overnight. It's a lot to take in. We can't be positive the deaths are some kind of revenge by these Gromleys, but we can't say they aren't. We must tread carefully."

"Revenge makes the most sense," Uncle Laird said. "I agree with Anderson. We need to come up with a plan." He looked straight at Tory. "I heard that you and Kenton Forrester are close."

Heat raced up her face, but she couldn't point a finger at either of her cousins for blabbing. After all, she had been the one to tell them, yet she hadn't sworn them to secrecy. "We went out once or twice. I can reach out to him again to see what he knows about what Ophelia said. I believe he and his family have killed a few demons in their day."

Her uncle's eyes brightened. "Perhaps we could ask him to help us."

She bet Kenton would love nothing more than to have her owe him one. However, she couldn't put her feelings ahead of the lives of many. "I will ask him the next time I see him."

"Please do."

The group disbanded. Tory and Greer headed up to the roof to take flight home since it was past closing time. "What are you going to do on your day off tomorrow," Greer asked with too much cheer. "Try to find Kenton?"

Tory turned to face her. "Yes. I will stop by Angelique's and hope to speak with him, just like I was asked to."

"Are you saying you won't ask him what happened the other night?"

Tory didn't want to lie. "The topic might come up."

"If you think I am being too pushy, it's because I want you to be as happy as I am with Blake. Having a mate is the most wonderful experience in the world."

Tory leaned back. "Whoa. Stop there. What makes you think Kenton and I are mates?" Greer had hinted she thought they were, but she'd never come out and stated it.

"Just saying. Your scales flash whenever he is around. And when have you ever heard of a Forrester having a job in Edendale?"

"I figured he was either bored or he needed the money. I doubt he's here because of me. He doesn't even know me very well."

"You'd be surprised what the Forresters know about the Guardians. It's almost creepy how intuitive they are." Greer sighed. "All I'm saying is keep an open mind and give the guy a chance. Maybe he was scared that the sex was too good."

Tory chuckled. "A guy scared? I doubt that."

"What if he's worried that since he's a Fey and you aren't, that you won't accept him? Face it. The guy lives in a freaking forest, doesn't own a car, and only now has a job."

Tory had been so absorbed in what was going on around her that she hadn't thought about what he was dealing with. "You might be right." She hugged her cousin. "I'll try to keep an open mind."

Greer grinned. "Let me know how it works out."

They headed up to the rooftop. Greer shifted and took off, and Tory followed suit. As she neared her house, she was tempted to continue flying until she landed in the middle of the realm. Even if she were able to find the eternal flame though, there was no guarantee she'd find Kenton.

No, it would be better to have a soak in the tub and get a good night's sleep. Tomorrow, she'd figure out the next step.

AFTER DOING A lot of thinking last night, Kenton decided he was going to face Tory and confess everything to her. They'd made love, which meant she found him an acceptable partner—or so he wanted to believe. Bevon was not home when Kenton awoke, but in a way, he was glad. He didn't need his brother giving him relationship advice.

After changing into his Angelique's Coffee Shop shirt and jeans, he teleported to the alley behind the shop and remained invisible until he was certain no one was watching. After dropping his cloak, he stepped into the kitchen.

"Hello, Donald. How goes it?" Kenton was quite pleased with his ability to absorb the slang of the region.

"Good. Yourself? The customers treating you well?"

Kenton wasn't used to people asking him how he was doing. It was usually his job to make sure others were okay. "A few are impatient, but most are grateful. If they are cranky, a good cup of coffee and a pastry usually cures their ills." He smiled.

"Good to hear." Donald waved a spatula at him, nodded, and then went back to work.

Kenton passed through the swinging kitchen doors, rushed down the hallway, and then stepped behind the counter. He started his morning ritual of checking the level of the coffee grounds in each of the machines and then made sure the condiments were all topped off. Lastly, he wiped down all of the tables in his section, getting ready for the morning rush. He couldn't imagine what his parents would say if they saw him doing menial chores. If they'd asked, he would have told them that it actually relaxed him since it gave him time to think.

Angelique clapped her hands, signaling the doors were about to open. Within a minute, half the seats were taken. While he knew it was Tory's day off, he doubted she'd stop in, and he couldn't blame her. He'd made a huge mistake by teleporting out of her house after they'd made love, but he had his reasons for leaving, which hopefully she would understand.

If he had stayed after their amazing lovemaking, he might have told her he was really good at reading people. From the way she rushed down the hallway, it was evident that Tory wasn't quite sure about him, and he wanted to give her time to think things through. It was for the best—or so he wanted to believe. Kenton rarely doubted himself, but he'd never made love to his mate before either.

If she didn't stop into the shop today, he'd seek her out after work. Kenton mentally tried to be ready for every kind of reaction. He hadn't been around her enough to know how she'd deal with his disappearing act or the flowers.

"Kenton?" Angelique called.

He jerked back to reality. "Coming!"

As he approached his boss, she nodded to a booth in back. "Someone has requested your presence." From the slight smile, he could guess who it was, though he couldn't believe he hadn't sensed Tory.

"Thank you."

Kenton spun around and made a beeline to her table. "Tory. Am I glad to see you."

"Really?"

Okay, this wasn't going to be easy. He shouldn't be surprised that the independent woman would respond with a bit of disdain. "We need to talk. About a lot of things."

"I came to talk too, but this place seems to be hopping. How about you get me a coffee with cream and a croissant, and maybe we can meet tonight at my place to discuss these things?"

When her lips quirked upward a bit, his heart soared. "That is perfect. I totally agree that this isn't exactly the safest place to talk." About the demons, about him running out on her, or about how he felt.

"I agree, but I had no other way of communicating with you except to come here. If you would get a cell phone, it would be easier."

"Like I said, the reception in the forest is spotty." He'd used that line often.

"If you had a phone, you could use it when you came to work."

"You're right." Either he needed one or it was time to give her the communication bracelet. He turned and rushed to prepare her order. As soon as he filled up her cup and poured in the cream, he carried it over to her. "Your croissant is heating."

She reached out and clasped his hand. "Thank you for the flowers."

Heat actually rushed up his face, and Kenton believed he was blushing—something he had never experienced before. "They are a small present to say I'm sorry for disappearing. It's one of the things I'd like to discuss with you tonight."

"It's a date."

Chapter Twelve

TORY CHANGED HER clothes three times for her date before deciding on a loose-fitting dress. She had yet to figure out how she wanted this evening to end, but should it go the same way as their last date, wearing something easy to remove would be best.

She had been a little angry at Kenton, but the moment he'd turned around and hurried toward her at the coffee shop, she forgave him. The lines around his eyes had appeared deeper, as if he hadn't slept much either.

To save time when Kenton arrived, she typed up and then printed off the information Ophelia had told them. Either Kenton would say all of that was new to him, or he'd be able to add some valuable information. Mostly, the Guardians needed to figure out how to rid Tarradon of these demons, assuming there was more than one of them.

A knock sounded on her door. How sweet. Kenton could have just as easily appeared in her living room, but this way was more proper. She pulled open the door and stared.

He wasn't wearing his coffee shop uniform like she assumed he would. Instead, he was dressed in black jeans and a rather form-fitting white T-shirt. While his attire was simple, it was sexy as hell. "Hey, come in," she managed to say.

From behind his back, he handed her a bottle of wine and a box. "I'm not sure this could make up for my mistake the other night, but I didn't know how else to say I'm sorry."

Tory never expected him to come with gifts. "You don't have to keep giving me presents." The man was sweet in his naiveté.

He lifted a shoulder. "The wine I thought we could share. As for the chocolates, maybe I could beg you for a taste."

His double-entendre wasn't lost on her, and she couldn't help but smile. "I'll get the wine opener."

This time, she didn't want to make love in the kitchen. Being in the bedroom would give her so much more room to explore him. As she retrieved two glasses, he opened the wine.

"I know you want to know why I left," he said.

Tory was thrilled she didn't have to ask him about it first. "I do. I'm aware that you live a rather sheltered life, but running out on a woman, especially after making love, is not cool in any realm."

"Trust me, Bevon explained that to me in no uncertain terms."

She tossed him a quick smile. "Remind me to thank Bevon. He seems like a man of reason."

"Sometimes. Anyway, I left because I sensed your hesitation about what we did, and I was trying to save you the embarrassment of having to tell me that sleeping with me had been a mistake. I honestly wasn't in a place to hear that."

"For real?" It stunned her that he had sensed her emotions, but also that he feared rejection.

"Yes. Why else would I leave?"

She studied him. Kenton really didn't seem to have a clue. "I came up with many scenarios, but apparently I didn't guess the right one." Tory nodded to the bottle. "How about pouring us a glass and then sit in the living room? I have some news."

"All's forgiven?" he asked, sounding relieved.

"Yes. I, for one, appreciate honesty more than anything."

He saluted her. "Roger that."

"Where did you learn that expression?" she asked.

"I overheard someone in the coffee shop say it. I've picked up a ton of phrases while working there."

Only Kenton would do that. "Good to know."

"I am curious. Why did you think I'd left?" he'd asked.

"You were scared? Or you could read minds. Or…"

He chuckled. "I get it. My actions defied reason. And you'd be right. It won't happen again. I promise."

Relief rushed through her. "Thank you."

They carried their drinks to the living room where he sat next to her on the couch. Tory scooted a few inches away from him. She had business to discuss and didn't need the intense distraction. Her body was already heating up from being so close. From the coffee table, she picked up the story she'd printed out about the Gromleys.

"The Guardians had a late-night meeting last night with someone from Earth. She apparently used to live in Tarradon and was aware of these demons."

"Was it Ophelia? The Faiten sisters' grandmother?"

Tory's jaw dropped. "You know her?"

"We've met a time or two. She is amazing."

Tory handed him the paper. "She is. I wrote down what she told us. I didn't want to forget anything."

Kenton read it. "Wow. I had heard rumors to this effect, but I wasn't aware that white lighters sent them away."

Darn. She was hoping he knew more. "I kind of feel sorry for them. Just because they are different doesn't mean they should be killed or banished to another realm—unless they took their anger out on people. Then all bets are off."

Kenton twisted toward her and lifted her chin. "I totally agree. The two groups should have tried to work together somehow." He inhaled. "You know, you should have been in charge of the world back then. I bet it would be a different place today."

While she appreciated the compliment, it held quite a lot of sadness. "Are you telling me your kind wasn't always welcomed here?" Or had she misread him?

"At some point in our history I think that was the case. It was why we formed our own realm. Even now, it's why we keep a low profile. Not to mention, we need to remain near the portals to keep them protected."

"And yet you spend most of your time in town now. Why is

that?"

He grinned. "I…ah…"

She held up a hand. "Never mind. We'll table that for another discussion, but I'm curious about something. The Guardians can create a portal wherever we are. Can you?"

From the way his chest slightly deflated, he was relieved she'd let him off the hook with her last question.

"Yes, but once we enter, it collapses. We aren't worried about anyone following us through those. It's the general portals that concern us."

"That's exactly what we face." Tory tapped the paper. "Which brings us back to this. Considering the Gromleys of old had their throats cut, and five recent people had their throats cut, do you think this could be a case of revenge?"

"It's a stretch but a definite possibility."

"Even if we learn the real reason for the attacks, that doesn't help us figure out how to stop them," she said.

Her cell rang, but she chose to ignore it. She wanted to get to know the real Kenton Forrester and not just in a sexual way. Her body, however, was going crazy, and her dragon was demanding satisfaction.

Stop it, she said. *I need to be sure my attraction wasn't just because I liked his looks.*

He's your mate, her dragon shot back.

"Aren't you going to answer it?" Kenton asked, nodding to the phone. If he hadn't sounded so concerned, she would have ignored it.

"I can do that." Tory picked it up, expecting it to be Greer. Instead it was her cousin Logan. He rarely called. "I should take this." She swiped the phone. "Hey, Logan."

"I have some news on the possible suicide killer."

Her heart skipped a beat. "Can I put you on speaker? Kenton is with me."

"Absolutely."

She pressed the button. "Okay, tell me."

"I decided to do a very deep dive on the five murdered victims. I wasn't sure what I was looking for, but when I couldn't find a connection between them, I went deeper."

Sometimes Logan could draw out the conclusion. "What's the bottom line?"

"I did a family tree for all of them. All of them came from two families—the Protero and the Colton families."

"What does this have to do with the Gromleys?"

"Both families were powerful white lighters. While the information from four hundred years ago is rather spotty, I was able to piece together a few things. There were records kept of their council meetings. Apparently, they went on record saying the Gromleys had to be destroyed and sent off this realm."

She sucked in a breath. "And you think these current day people are being targeted as a way to pay for their ancestors sending the Gromleys to Cargonia?"

"Draw your own conclusions, but that is what I get out of it."

Kenton leaned closer. "Kenton here. Did you learn if anyone else was responsible for their demise? I'm wondering if maybe the Feys either helped the Gromleys or helped the locals get rid of them."

"I don't know, but I did recognize one name from back then—someone who was the head of the council."

Now he had her curious. "Who?"

"Tory's grandfather, Altus Sinclair."

Her pulse raced. "What are you saying? That the Guardians helped kill the Gromleys?"

"It's possible, which means your family and maybe mine could be the next target."

TORY HUNG UP, her face pale and a bit contorted. Drat. Kenton was actually scared for her and her family. Why he thought this Gromley demon would target her specifically, he didn't know, but Kaleena had Finn to help protect her, and both Nessa and Greer also had mates, assuming the Caspians were included in this vendetta.

"I have a suggestion," he said as calmly as he could.

Her face hardened as she put down the phone and turned her attention back to him. "Unless you know how to locate this demon, what can you do?"

"I can keep you safe."

She looked at him like he had two heads. "How? You said it takes your whole family to create this magic ball that might kill a demon. This guy figured out a way for five people to kill themselves in their homes!"

"That is true, but if you aren't on Tarradon, they can't find you."

She scrunched her brows. "I'm not sure I follow."

"Come to Feyrion with me." He held his breath.

Tory huffed out a laugh. "Seriously? Not only do I have a job, but as a Guardian, I have to protect the people here. I won't run off because I'm in danger."

He crossed his arms over his chest. "How are you going to protect others? Can you be sure this demon can't convince you to slit your throat?"

"Slitting my throat won't kill me."

"Okay, if he can tell you're a shifter, he might compel you to stab yourself in that soft spot below your heart."

Her mouth opened. "You have a terrible imagination."

Kenton clasped her hand. "Would you mind coming to the forest with me for a few minutes then? I want to ask Fay something. The Fairies are intuitive. She might know something."

"You haven't told her about the Gromleys?"

"I have, but that was before I was aware you might be in danger. I'm hoping she can offer a suggestion. I'll bring you back here whenever you want."

Tory pressed her lips together. "Okay, but how are we getting there? I can't teleport."

He smiled. "Like this."

One second, they were in her living room and the next in Fay's house. To be precise, it was Fay, Meena, and Tally's house.

Tory grabbed his arm. "Holy crap. Did you just teleport me to the forest?"

From the sparkle in her eyes, she liked it. "Yes."

"Where are we?"

"At my house." Fay said as she exited her bedroom. "This is a surprise, brother. I can feel Tory's concern and excitement blended together."

"Fay!" Tory said. "That's because I've never teleported before."

Kenton needed to explain things quickly. "Logan Caspian did some research. We have reason to believe that Gromley demons might be coming after the Guardians next."

Fay sucked in a breath. "That is not good."

"Exactly." He told her what he'd learned. "Any suggestions?"

"I suggest you tell Tory everything and let her decide what to do next."

His mate glanced up at him. "What do you mean everything? What haven't you told me?"

He turned to face his sister. "Thanks for the tactful suggestion."

She smiled sweetly. "You were taking your sweet time. I was just giving you the needed nudge."

Tory clasped his arm. "I'll ask again. What aren't you telling me?"

"Let's go to my place. I'm hoping Bevon is still out. I'll explain everything there."

"I prefer you take me back to my place."

He didn't want to piss her off more than he already had. "If you wish."

Kenton placed a hand on her back and teleported them to her home. She placed a hand on the back of the sofa. It was almost as if she was testing whether they really were in her house. "That was too strange. I feel as if I'm in a dream."

He walked over to the kitchen, grabbed the half empty bottle of wine and then returned to the living room. "I have a feeling we'll be needing this."

Without saying a word, he poured her a glass of wine and handed it to her. He then motioned they sit down.

Once she settled down, she tossed back most of her wine and then faced him. "I'm ready. Tell me."

"You remember Malpan, right?"

The chuckle that escaped wasn't from cheer. "That scum hurt a lot of people. Of course, I remember him."

"You recall that he hurt you too, and that Greer and Declan had to heal you."

"I don't need a rehash of my life."

"It was a lie." He waited for her to yell or something. Instead, she just stared at him.

"Which part?"

"Let me back up to right before Malpan attacked you. You were fighting some dragons and were injured enough to fall to the ground."

"That's not unusual in such a battle."

"What you don't know is that when Malpan realized I was a Fey, he knew he was about to die. Seconds before I tossed him through the portal where my guards were waiting to rip out his soul, he implanted part of his dark soul into you."

She sucked in a breath. "I had dark magic in me? Like Danita had?"

"Not quite. Most of the time, a dark Fey will put a dark spell on the person, like what he did to Danita. In your case, it was more serious. You had a kind of dark cancer, if you will, growing inside you."

She placed a hand on her chest. "But Greer and Declan did their magic and saved me."

"No. I'm afraid the darkness shut down your dragon's ability to save you. Greer and Declan wouldn't have been able to save you."

She shook her head. "But I'm still alive. Clearly, I didn't die."

"No. I was able to convince Griffin to let me take you to Feyrion and cure you."

"Griffin knew?"

"That's what you're getting out of this? Tory, you almost died. Hell, you did die for a few seconds."

She polished off her wine and set down her glass. "I don't understand any of this."

"Not that it is critical to the story since I might not have acted any differently, but from the moment I saw you flying overhead doing battle, I knew you were my mate."

She froze and stared at him. "Then it's true."

He shouldn't have thrown so much at her at once. She had yet to come to grips with what he had to do to save her. "Yes, but we can discuss what that means in a moment. Back on Feyrion, I had minutes to save you, so I took a piece of my life light and placed it in you."

When he nodded to her chest, she slapped her palm over her heart. "The heat? Those slight light pulses are you?"

He was relieved she understood. "Yes."

"Did that cure me?"

"Yes. It was able to dissolve, if that is even the right word, all of the darkness inside you. It took about a week for you to recover."

She placed her palms together and pressed her fingers to her lips. "I don't remember anything."

Now he needed to deliver the third blow—or was it the fourth? "With a little help, I was able to erase the memory of your time on Feyrion."

"You erased my memory? Are you kidding me?"

"Like I've said, I have many talents."

Chapter Thirteen

TORY'S MIND SEEMED to be spinning as she tried to absorb all of this new information. "Why didn't you tell me?" she asked. "I mean this happened a while ago."

"That's kind of the purpose of erasing your memory."

Her lips pressed together. "Why would you do that? Was there something on Feyrion I shouldn't have seen?"

"Not exactly, but after the attack, I made the call that you weren't ready to learn we were mates. Even if you hadn't been my mate, we would have erased your memory because we don't want other worlds to be aware of Feyrion."

"I'm sorry for being so dense, but what is on Feyrion that is so secret? Danita knows your realm exists. Why keep it from me?"

Kenton had more or less been waiting for these questions and had prepared his answer. "Our magic could be exploited if a lot of people learned about us."

She stared at him for a minute. "I can see your point about wanting to keep your talents secret. My family feels that if Tarradon learns who we are, we'd be taken advantage of. I imagine it's the same for you."

"Thank you." Kenton couldn't believe she was so forgiving—at least of that one part.

Tory twisted away from him and leaned back. "I can't believe some of my family members knew about this and covered it up."

"I asked them not to say anything. It was for your own good. I wanted to be the one to tell you—when the time was right."

Her lips pressed together. She faced him, her gaze not a forgiving one. "You didn't think to ask me what I wanted?"

"About what? Me inserting my light into you or erasing your memory?"

"Both, I guess."

"First off, you were dying and weren't exactly awake for me to ask you. Besides, you are my mate, and no matter what, I will do everything and anything to protect you—including keeping something secret from you until the time is right to tell you."

She sat up straighter. "Fine. Now that I know, I want this thing you put in my chest, out."

Tory couldn't be serious. "You don't understand."

Her eyebrows rose. "Enlighten me."

"For starters, removing my life light might kill you—assuming I could remove it. It's not something I've ever done before," Kenton explained.

"If you put it in, you can take it out." Tory dipped her chin. "Please remember that I was quite healthy before Malpan came along. I am fully healed now, so I don't need it."

"It will give you strength."

"Look. Right now, I don't want to be artificially connected to you, and I mean that in the nicest way. If we do end up together, I want it to be because we want to be together, not because some light is making us."

Blood pounded in his ears, and his gut was churning something fierce. He held up a hand, needing a moment to think. Tory was his mate. She couldn't really mean that she wanted his light out of her. "I get it, but you need to give me some time to figure out how to undo it. I need to find out if it will harm *me*." That was a low blow, but Kenton was desperate. He couldn't lose their connection.

"Fine. While you are figuring things out—and I'm figuring things out—I'd like you to leave."

"Leave? No." He clasped her hands in his. "Tory, we belong together. Just give me time to prove it."

"Do you really think a relationship should be based on lies

though? Has there been anything you've told me that was the truth?"

Her anger actually hurt his whole body. "Yes. I want to be with you. You do things to me that no other woman has. And that's the truth."

"This is all about you?"

"Ouch." He released his grip and stabbed a hand through his hair, but his fingers only tangled it more. "No. That's not it. I am devastated that I handled everything so poorly."

She stood. "I need time to think. Not only did you implant something in my body and erase my memory, you asked my family to keep it from me. I'm betting you didn't just happen to run into me the day I was on my way to see my sister."

He wouldn't lie. "No. I knew who you were."

"Yet, you pretended as if we were strangers," she said.

"If I had told you everything while you were doubled over in pain, I don't think it would have gone over well."

Her shoulders sagged. "Okay, I'll give you that, but I'm over-whelmed right now. Please go."

"Fine, but this is far from over."

Knowing when he'd overstayed his welcome, he teleported back to his house. Damn, Fay. He should have known better than to tell Tory they were fated mates when her cousin had just warned her some maniac was out for revenge against the Guardians. If there was a class on how to be tactful, he'd sign up in a heartbeat. The big issue was how would she react when she learned what his mother had done to her?

TORY PACED THE living room, unable to understand it all. She and Kenton were mates. Her dragon had told her that several times, and her body responded to him so much that she had to believe it was true.

But Kenton put some part of himself inside her. Maybe that had made her believe they were destined for one another.

Nope, the sexual and emotional draw is there. No doubt about it, her dragon said with authority.

Her inner animal had never been known for her superior intellect. *If he erased my memory once, what's to say he isn't compelling me now to believe him? Huh? Answer that!*

Whoa. Calm down. If he compelled you to do anything, you wouldn't be questioning it.

Maybe you're right, she telepathed.

Damn. This kind of speculation served no purpose. Deep down, Tory knew Kenton and she were mates. Why wipe her memory though? Eventually, he'd take her back to his realm. She'd see everything then.

If she was going to figure anything out, Tory needed another drink. The fact that her family knew things, and had kept it from her, possibly pissed her off more than Kenton withholding information. Her hand went to her heart, wondering what exactly he had put inside her. Magic? Or was it some physical piece? He called it his life light. If it were truly light, would it even stay inside a person for long?

Tory looked around for her glass to see if she'd finished it. As much as she was tempted to call Greer and ask her to come over, her cousin had been involved in the cover up. She needed someone else. Someone rational and logical. Camden! The scientist would be level-headed and would tell her the truth.

She picked up her phone and dialed his number.

"Tory, what's wrong?" he asked.

"Where are you?"

"Huh?"

"Are you home?" she asked.

"Yes," Camden said.

"Can I come over? I really need to talk to someone."

He hesitated before answering. "Sure. I'm working in the basement. I'll leave the front door open."

Camden spent much of his time down there working on his projects. What that boy needed was a mate, but how would he ever find one if he didn't venture far from his two labs? She inhaled. Matchmaking wasn't what she needed to be worrying about right now.

After grabbing an unopened bottle of wine, Tory stepped outside, shifted, and flew to Camden's home. He lived in a rather rundown house about five miles from town. He'd purchased it because the basement was huge, and it would allow him to do his experiments.

She must not have been paying attention, because she barely remembered flying. Once there, she shifted back and rushed up to the unlocked front door. Inside, she headed to the basement. The stairwell was barely lit, and the basement wasn't much better, but that was Camden. Her cousin was a genius—and logical to a fault.

No surprise, he was bent over a microscope. Being a dragon shifter, he would be aware she was there, so she waited until he finished what he was doing.

Camden held up a finger. "Just one sec."

"Take your time."

Tory let him work. She walked around his lab, not making sense of most of it. He stood up and faced her. "What can I do for you? I don't have any additional information about the Gromleys if that is why you are here."

"I'm not here about that. Can we go upstairs and talk?" She waved a bottle of wine.

"Whoa. It must be serious. Let me wash my hands."

He stepped over to the sink and cleaned up. Once he was done, he motioned they go upstairs where she followed him into the old kitchen. Not only could it use a good cleaning, it would greatly benefit from a major upgrade. Who was she to judge though? As long as he was happy, she was good with it.

Camden opened the wine without asking any questions. When he handed her the glass, he finally faced her. "Spill."

"Can we sit?"

"Sure."

Tory plucked a T-shirt from the chair and set it next to Camden on the sofa. "Did you know that Malpan had infected my body with a part of his soul and that your brother allowed Kenton to take me to Feyrion to be healed?"

Camden tossed back part of his wine. "I'd heard rumors."

Yet he'd said nothing. "Did you also hear rumors that Kenton erased my memory of the whole event?"

Her cousin dragged a hand down his chin. "No, though I did find it odd that you seemed to have blocked everything out. I figured it was your way of coping."

"Yet you never thought to say anything?"

One brow cocked. "It wouldn't be my place. Plus, Kenton did you a favor—and us—by saving your life. Ask Danita. She watched you almost die right there in the woods."

This was bad. "I didn't know Danita saw what happened."

"Yup. It was why Griffin was there. He was impossible to talk to during the time you were in Feyrion. He was convinced he'd sealed your death. He even flew to the eternal flame to demand answers. Apparently, Fay, or maybe it was another sister, told him that all would be well. Eventually, Kenton showed up and said you were back in your bed." Camden smiled. "I don't see what the big deal is. You're here, and you're healed."

Camden was usually more sympathetic than that. "I get that, but everyone lied. I don't even want to know if my parents knew."

He held up his hands. "Did it ever occur to you that they believed you needed time to come to grips with the fact you'd been infected by a dark Fey?"

Now he sounded like Kenton. "Maybe. Or else it was the fact that I needed time to come to grips with the concept of Kenton giving me part of his soul to save me." He had never called his life light a soul, but it seemed like a good name for it. If the dark Fey could implant part of his inner being into her, Kenton could do the same.

Camden's eyes widened. "He implanted something inside you?"

"Yes. I don't know how he did it, but part of him is in me."

He grimaced. "I'd be a little squibbed out about that too."

"Right?"

Camden drank his wine. "Just so you know, I wasn't aware he did anything of the sort. I swear."

"He might not have told anyone." Her family might only be guilty of telling her who had healed her. "It gets better. We are mates."

His eyes lit up. "That's fantastic." He quickly sobered. "From the lack of excitement, you don't think it's so fantastic? You seem really stressed out. Since you came here, I'm guessing you want a sounding board from someone who would use a clinical approach."

"You're right."

He finished off his wine. Needing to keep up, she tossed back half the glass in two gulps.

"As I see it, everyone was right in keeping you in the dark. At the time, you weren't able to handle being with a Fey," Camden said.

Was that true? Tory was usually the one to stay calm, but now she was totally unglued. "Maybe you're right."

"I'm a scientist. I have to be right."

That made her laugh. "Since when did you become so egotistical?"

"Ouch. I made you smile, didn't I?"

"You did."

Camden swung his body around and plopped his feet on the sofa. "What's your next move? It seems like your Fey man is good at giving you space. It's like he trusts you to make the right decision."

She wasn't sure about that. Right now, her ability to make good decisions seemed to be lacking. "When he dropped the bomb about erasing my memory and then told me he was my mate, I don't think I reacted rationally."

"You think?"

She dipped her chin. "Fine. I didn't handle it well. What would you have done?"

"I would have holed up in my lab and worked on something fun."

"I can't hide. Sure, I'd like to spend a few days designing jewelry for you to make, but that is not an option. There are demons out there killing people."

Camden's feet hit the floor so hard, the room shook. "You are to stay away from them."

She held up her free hand. "I get it. They are dangerous." She told him what Logan said about those victims being part of a family who drove the demons to Cargonia.

He whistled. "I might want revenge too. I don't know much about Cargonia, but it might not be the nicest place to live."

"I'm thinking you might be right." Even though Finn's friend Zane Barrows came from there, what good would it do to learn how hard life on Cargonia had been? The Gromleys might or might not have deserved such treatment, but she couldn't do anything about it now.

A loud pop sounded in his basement, and Camden jerked. "Oh shit. I forgot I have something cooking."

"Go take care of it." She stood and hugged him. "Thank you."

"You'll do the right thing. Eventually."

"Thanks for the vote of confidence. Take care of your lab. You don't need to burn down your house."

Camden rushed off, and Tory left. She wasn't in the mood to go home though. A good stiff drink would do wonders for her. Tomorrow, she'd deal with Kenton Forrester.

Chapter Fourteen

"SHE KICKED ME out," Kenton told his brother. "I should have stayed, but Tory was not happy when I told her everything."

"She was upset when you explained how you'd saved her life?" Bevon asked.

"I honestly can't remember which upset her more—the fact we erased her memory without her permission, asked her family to keep my secret, put my life light inside her to save her, or that we are mates."

Bevon whistled. "You told her all of that at once?" Bevon shook his head as he headed into the kitchen. Kenton followed.

In retrospect, he should have eased her into all of the deception. "I had to. She kept asking questions. At least I didn't tell her what our mother did to her."

Bevon pulled out two beers from the fridge and handed him one. "Thank goodness for small favors. What is your next move?"

"Tory seems to need time to absorb all this information. I'll keep a watch on her without her knowledge."

Bevon leaned against the counter. "You're worried about the Gromley coming after her, aren't you?"

"Yes. If any of these Gromleys are willing to kill five people whose ancestors harmed them, they won't hesitate to seek vengeance against the Guardians." Kenton tossed back some beer. "The more I think about it, the more convinced I am that the Fairies were involved somehow. It might have been their spell that caused the Gromleys to be kicked off of Tarradon."

"We usually don't interfere with the running of this realm."

"True, but it's possible Gromleys once existed on Feyrion. We might have had a history with them—a not very good one."

Bevon hopped up on the counter. "I don't recall hearing much about them, but our mother would know."

"If that's the case, I should take a trip there. I need to explain how I messed up with Tory."

Bevon hissed in a breath. "You probably don't want to do that. Mom expects you and Tory to mate. If you tell her you might have ruined things between you two, she might lock you away for life." His brother grinned.

"Don't smile at me. If I'm not around, then you'd have to be king, and your fun, carefree life would be over."

Bevon immediately sobered. "Good point. How about I go to Feyrion and ask around about these demons? I too want to know what we are up against."

Relief poured out of Kenton. "That would be great. In the meantime, I'll keep a low profile and see what my mate is up to."

"If she catches you, you'll never get Tory to change her mind about you."

Kenton grunted. "I know I fucked up."

"Royally. Pun intended."

No proper Royal would make that kind of error. "I'll be careful, and thanks for checking out the history of these demons."

"Anything to get you mated and out of the house. I'm ready to be on my own after a few hundred years."

Kenton gave Bevon his middle finger even though his brother was only kidding. They could have created another house at any time, but Kenton and Bevon enjoyed being with each other—or so he believed.

ONCE MORE THE flight from Camden's house to the top of the Wings Bar seemed super quick. Tory needed to focus on what she was doing. If not, she could possibly end up being harmed by some stupid Gromley demon.

Before she knew it, she'd landed, shifted, and then hurried down the two flights to the main floor. That was odd. Either someone had altered time, or Tory's ability to focus had collapsed. She inwardly chuckled. It was like someone was erasing her memory on how she moved from one place to another.

Tory glanced around the bar. Even though it was a weekday, Wings was hopping. Good. The noise would help block out some of her swirling thoughts.

About five bar seats near the entrance were vacant. She sat down, placed her purse on the counter, and checked to see who was bartending. Seeing her sister's mate, Finn, reduced her stress by tenfold. Unburdening to him, however, was not an option. He'd tell Kaleena, and her twin had enough to deal with considering she'd just given birth to Sapphire.

Finn looked up and smiled. As soon as he finished with a customer, he came over. "Hey. You're here alone?"

The last time she'd been there, she'd been with Kenton. "Yup. Can I have a Light Kegger and an order of potato skins?"

For some reason, that combination sounded like the perfect pick-me-up.

"Coming right up!"

Tory wanted to drown her sorrows, but her dragon would never let her get sufficiently drunk for that.

"You look like you could use a drink?" said a voice she'd never heard before.

Not one to be rude, she swung around to face the newcomer. Whoa. His eyes were almost iridescent, and the slight scruff on his face looked good on him. Not that she was interested in anyone but Kenton but for some reason having a stranger to talk to might be just what she needed.

"You're right. It's why I ordered one," she said with as much cheer as possible.

He slid his tall frame onto the seat and held out his hand. "I'm Malakai, but my friends call me Kai."

"Hi, Kai. I'm Tory." She liked that they didn't exchange last names. Sinclair was too well-known around here.

Finn set a beer in front of her, and when he faced Kai, Finn's usual happy go lucky attitude disappeared. Okay, that was odd.

"What can I get you?" Finn asked.

"The same as what Tory is having."

While it was subtle, Finn raised a concerned brow, but she felt no need to explain why she was talking to a stranger.

"You got it." Finn faced her. "Skins will be up in a sec."

"Thanks." She turned to the handsome stranger. "Are you new in town?"

Okay, it might be dumb to talk to a stranger at a bar, but it wasn't as if she'd leave with him. Between her dragon skills, along with Finn's, they'd be able to handle him, not that he seemed the violent type. It wasn't as if he was one of the Gromley demons. She would have sensed something if he had been, or so she wanted to believe.

His eyes turned a shade darker. "Yes."

O-kay. She thought he'd elaborate, but since she wasn't planning on divulging any of her secrets, she didn't feel the need to press this guy for information. "What brings you to Edendale?"

"I'm trying to connect with some family. It's been a long time since I've been around them."

She sighed. "I wish you luck. Almost all of my relatives live here in Edendale. It's nice to have them so close, but sometimes I wonder what it would be like to live somewhere else, where no one knows my name." Tory almost chuckled. Clearly, she'd been watching too many television shows from Earth.

Finn delivered Kai's drink. "Want to run a tab?"

"Sure."

Finn turned to her. "Are you okay?"

He'd never asked her before. Surely, he didn't think this guy would try anything. He wasn't a shifter, so if she felt uncomfortable, all she had to do was head up to the roof top and fly home. She made an effort to smile. "Never better. Thanks for asking."

As soon as Finn returned to the other end of the bar, Kai lifted his beer and took a sip. "The bartender seems upset over something."

"He's my twin sister's mate. They just had a baby a few days ago. I'm betting he hasn't slept in days."

"Ah, a baby." He sounded wistful. "I can't imagine what it would be like to be a dad."

"That's far off on my horizon too."

Kai held up his glass. "To Edendale and to family."

That was a nice toast. "To family."

He sipped his beer and didn't say anything for a bit. "You seem sad, Tory."

Was it that obvious? She thought her smile and upbeat tone to Finn had covered it up. "I just had a fight with my boyfriend. He lied to me, and I'm trying to figure out what to do about it. Walk out or forgive him?"

"Ouch. I understand lies. For years my family told us stories about my grandparents and what kind of people they were. When I learned the truth, I was enraged."

"Your grandparents weren't good people?"

"On the contrary. They were amazing, hard-working people, going about their daily lives. Then the town elders came to them and said they wanted the land my grandparents were living on—land they that owned."

"That's terrible. What did they do?"

"They fought back. Apparently, it was ugly."

"I've heard that happens often on Earth. Big cities pop up, and if you don't do what they want, you lose. Sure, they are willing to buy the land, but some things can't be bought for money."

"Wow. I'm glad you understand."

She nodded. "What was the lie you were told?"

His lips thinned. "I was told my grandparents were mauled to death by some animals. My mom was about ten and had to be raised by other families."

"I am so sorry. Is she still alive?"

"Yes, but I don't remember her ever being happy. The death of her parents still traumatizes her."

"She had you."

He smiled and drank most of his beer. "She did, but then she became barren. I always thought it was the stress."

"And your dad?" Tory shouldn't have probed, but there was something about his story that touched her.

"He hasn't been in the picture since I was about five."

That was tragic. "Who are you trying to connect with here?"

"I'm trying to find some long-lost cousins." He looked away for a moment, but then turned back to her. "Enough about my story. I should be cheering you up."

She smiled. "I'll be fine. I just need to figure out my next move, that's all."

Finn stopped by and slid the potato skins in front of her. Tory wasn't in the mood to drown her sorrows anymore. Needing to pay and leave, she reached for her purse. She must not have been paying attention, because she knocked it off the counter. It fell, but before it could hit the floor, she'd actually caught it. "What the—"

Tory lifted the purse onto the counter, reached inside, and handed Finn her card.

"Nice catch," Kai said.

Tory was equally surprised that she had. She had great reflexes, but they weren't *that* fast. "Thank you."

"Are you sure you're okay. You seem particularly bothered."

She forced a smile, because this guy was beginning to get on her nerves. "Like I said, I need time to figure out how to handle my boyfriend." She wasn't about to tell Kai that Kenton and she had only known each other for a short while.

With as much energy and cheer as she could muster, Tory ate her skins and polished off her drink. Once she finished, she faced

Kai. "I should go. I hope you connect with your family."

"Thanks. Can I walk you out?"

"I'm good."

Before he made a big deal of it, she raced to the back, climbed the stairs to the roof and took off.

While Tory enjoyed talking to Kai—at least at first—something regarding the warping of time was happening to her. While she had no proof, she was beginning to think it had something to do with Kenton's life light that was inside her. Until she could nail down what it was that was different, she'd keep her suspicions to herself.

Tory had just walked into her house when her cell rang, and her stomach instantly tightened. Who would call this late at night? She pulled out her cell from her purse. Oh, no.

"What is it, Mom?" Tory asked.

"It's your father. He's taken a turn for the worse."

That made no sense. "Hold on. I thought you said he was just tired."

"I thought that too, but even though he's been sleeping, he isn't improving."

"Did you call Greer or Declan?"

"Yes, but they have no idea what is wrong with him."

Tory wasn't a healer. For some reason, her mind shot to those five dead people, along with the notion that these Gromleys were out for revenge against the original families who drove them out as well as the Guardians who had helped them. "What can I do?"

"Greer suggested I speak with Logan. I did, and he seems to think this might be an attack by the Gromley demons."

"Oh, no. I'll be right over. We'll figure something out."

"Hurry, dear."

Chapter Fifteen

H AD IT BEEN supremely stupid to enter Wings in his invisible form in order to spy on his mate? Yes, but Kenton had to see for himself what Tory's state of mind was in. If she went to a bar to drink—alone—then she was upset.

When he spotted that stranger sitting next to her, he nearly lost it. If Finn hadn't been there to keep an eye on Tory, Kenton might have pretended to stop by to grab a beer. Whether Tory would have bought his excuse was the big question.

Kenton didn't stay long or get too close to either of them, because he couldn't be sure if she could sense his presence—invisible or not. If Tory learned he'd been spying on her, the damage to their relationship would have been irreparable.

To make certain she remained safe from any demons, he stayed outside until he saw her take off from the rooftop. For his peace of mind, he teleported to her house and beat her there by several minutes. It was only when she landed and went inside that Kenton breathed a sigh of relief.

Just as he was about to teleport back home, Tory exited and took off again. Where in the realm would she be going at this hour? Either she had some secret rendezvous with the stranger, or something was wrong. In either case, he needed to find out.

While Kenton couldn't fly, he could watch where she was headed and then teleport to that location. Repeating the process a few times would allow him to follow her. When Tory landed at a large home in an expensive neighborhood, he hid close by. He wasn't sure who lived in the grand house, but considering its size, it might belong to her parents. Normally, Kenton would be fine knowing that she was visiting her parents, but the late hour concerned him. He somehow doubted she'd be talking about her problems this late at night.

As much as he wanted to cloak himself and teleport inside so he could listen, his moral compass told him to leave, that this was a private matter between Tory and her folks. Even if some relative didn't live there, it didn't belong to a demon.

Once or twice in the past when he'd been spying, he'd lost his ability to remain cloaked, and he couldn't chance that happening again.

The dilemma was that if Tory, or someone she loved was in trouble, and she needed to get ahold of him, she wouldn't be able to. Who would she call then? He mentally snapped his fingers. Finn. His shift probably hadn't ended, which made what Kenton had in mind perfect.

If only he had a cell phone, things would be different. He hadn't been lying when he said the reception in the forest was spotty. It was, but that didn't mean he couldn't have one when he was in town.

Kenton teleported to the rooftop of Wings. He doubted anyone would question how he'd been able to reach the roof, considering he wasn't a dragon shifter, but he'd have a smaller chance of being spotted this way.

Inside, Finn was still working. Good. Whatever the emergency at the Sinclair home—assuming that was where Tory was—it wasn't bad enough for them to need him.

"Hey, Finn," Kenton said as he slid onto a barstool.

"Kenton! You just missed Tory."

"That so?" Kenton was glad the man who'd been trying to ingratiate himself into her life wasn't there.

"What can I get you?"

"A beer."

Finn smiled. He poured the drink and placed it on the counter in front of Kenton. "Did something happen today between you and

Tory? She seemed a bit upset."

Kenton appreciated that Tory came to a safe place to have a drink. She probably knew Finn's schedule. Unfortunately, this wasn't the best place to discuss their problems, but he figured he could be discreet. "I told Tory the truth about the Malpan situation and her little trip to my homeland."

Finn whistled. "Ah, so that was what had her upset."

Kenton huffed out a laugh. "Yes. Did she say anything to you?"

"No. Tory is not a complainer. She'll keep her problems to herself." Finn's cell rang. "Hold on. It's my mate." He turned his back to the bar. "Hey, can't sleep? Whoa, slow down. Your dad?" Finn spun around. "As a matter of fact, I do. Kenton is sitting right here. Of course. I can get someone to cover the rest of my shift. No babe, you stay home with Sapphire. I will call you as soon as I know anything. Love you too." Finn disconnected.

"What is it?" Kenton asked.

Finn looked around. "Apparently, Kaleena's father is ill. Neither Greer nor Declan were able to heal him. Tory thought you might be able to help."

It thrilled him that Tory would let him near her father. Maybe all was not lost between them. "I'd be happy to try. Where do they live?" He wasn't about to admit he might know the location.

"Give me a sec."

He rushed over to the other bartender and returned quickly. "I'm going with you. It will be easier than drawing a map. Did you drive?"

"No."

"Mind flying?"

If it meant he could help Tory, he'd do anything. "Not at all."

They rushed up to the roof where Finn shifted into his dragon form. A second later, Kenton was airborne. If neither Greer nor Declan could heal Tory's dad, and her dad's dragon couldn't help, either the man had been injured in battle or the demon had somehow found out who the Guardians were and come after him. It was possible that four or five hundred years ago, the Guardians hadn't kept their identity a secret.

Finn landed in the driveway and set Kenton down. At some point, Kenton would have to reveal to Tory's family his ability to teleport. To be fair to Finn, had Kenton been able to pay more attention, he might have enjoyed the flight a bit more. His thoughts had been solely on Tory and what she was going through right now.

Finn shifted back. "This way," he said as he jogged up the path to the mansion.

He knocked and an older woman answered. "Moira." He kissed her on the cheek. "How bad is it?"

She sniffled. "I don't know. I could tell he hasn't been himself this week, but Jamison kept telling me he just needed to rest. Today, he passed out, and now his lit dragon scales are fading. It doesn't look good."

Kenton's heart broke for not only Tory, but for her mother and the rest of the family.

Finn spun around. "This is Kenton. He's the one who saved—"

She held out her hand. "I know who he is. Thank you for saving my daughter."

"Of course."

"Jamison is on the living room couch. He still refuses to admit he is seriously ill, but after more than a hundred years, I can tell he's not right."

Kenton followed Tory's mom down a long hallway that opened up to a massive living room. Tory was on her knees in front of the sofa, holding her father's hand. She looked up and nodded. As much as he wanted to talk to her, now wasn't the time.

Both Greer and Declan were close by, as was another brother, who he'd not met.

"What can you tell me?" Kenton looked mostly at Tory.

"We don't know, and Dad insists he's fine."

"I'm just tired," her father said. "This isn't the first time I've been run down."

"The last time you were run down, you'd been in a battle in which a dragon shifter nicked your heart," Moira said.

Her dad didn't have a comeback.

Tory shifted her gaze from her dad back to Kenton. "I'm thinking maybe the Gromley demons are responsible."

"It's certainly possible. Let me see if I can identify the source, but to be truthful, this is something I usually let my sisters handle. They can do a spell to take care of what might ail him."

"But you cured Tory," her mother said.

"Yes, but she had been infected by a dark Fey, not a demon. Before I draw any conclusions though, let me see what the situation is here first."

Kenton knelt next to Tory and placed one hand on Mr. Sinclair's chest and the other on his forehead. Kenton closed his eyes and focused on finding the source of the evil. Because he believed it was a demon, he concentrated on the chemical compound the demon used to control the person's mind, but he detected nothing.

When Tory placed a hand on his shoulder, it was as if their powers united. Kenton moved the palm from Mr. Sinclair's cheek to his neck, and his other hand from his chest to his hip. The change caused an electric spark to flow through his body, and a signature appeared.

Kenton opened his eyes. "It appears as if Mr. Sinclair was infected by the Gromley demon."

Tory's eyes widened. "How? If what you say is true, why didn't my father cut his own throat?"

Since none of the family members asked about the identity of the demon, Tory must have filled them in—or else some other Guardian had.

Tory's tone held worry mixed with doubt, which caused a tremendous amount of anguish to build inside him. Kenton had to push that aside. Her father's health was in jeopardy. Kenton turned to her mom. "Did Logan tell you about these demons?"

"Yes. He warned us, but Jamison swears he didn't come in contact with anyone."

"Most people don't give a second thought when someone bumps into them. If this demon was out to destroy the Sinclairs, he could be cagey. Sir, have you been out and about anytime this week or last?"

"I went to the store with Moira about a week ago. Someone helped us with our groceries, but I didn't hug him or anything." He looked upward. "I also went to lunch with a friend the next day." His brows pinched. "Come to think of it though, when I was walking to a restaurant, someone came out of a side alley and bumped into me. He apologized profusely, and I went on my way. Do you think he could have been a demon? I didn't sense anything radiating off him."

"Do you remember what this man looked like?" Kenton asked.

"Good looking, I guess," her dad said. "Tall, broad shouldered, but he had strange eyes."

"Strange how?" Tory asked.

"They were like opals. Iridescent almost."

Tory stilled, and Kenton placed a hand on her shoulder. "What is it? Do you know him?"

Tory dropped back onto her haunches. "I might have met him at the bar tonight."

"The man you were talking to?" Finn asked.

"Yes."

Kenton hadn't sensed this man was a demon, but because Kenton was cloaked, it would have blocked his senses a bit. Not only that, jealousy had been raging through his body.

"Tory, he could have been a demon."

She shook her head. "He seemed too lost to be one."

Kenton didn't see how that eliminated him. "Was he angry?"

"He told me he'd come to town to look for some relatives, but I didn't get the sense he was out for revenge."

"What does this all mean?" Mrs. Sinclair asked. "What could a demon do to us?"

Kenton was through with lying. "If this demon touched your husband, I fear he might be in trouble."

As expected, several of them talked at once. Finally, Kenton had to hold up his hand. "I understand your concern, but I have a plan."

Tory touched his arm, and he turned to face her. "If this man was a demon, why didn't he compel my father to kill himself?" she asked.

"Just like those other five victims," Tory's mom added.

Kenton couldn't be sure, but he had a suspicion. "Is it possible the Guardians are immune to suggestion? We Feys are." He looked at Mr. Sinclair. "You didn't have any compulsion—"

"To kill myself? No. We have a lot of magic inside us that helps to protect us from stuff like that."

"Good," Kenton said. They could discuss the demon later. Right now, Tory's father needed his help. "I would like to ask my sisters to help. I believe they have the magic to remove this demonic influence." He wasn't sure how else to explain it.

"Do you think if we took a sample of his blood that we would find the same chemical the other victims had inside of them?" Tory asked.

"I suspect the answer is yes."

"I thought you lived in the middle of the realm," her dad said. "I'm not sure I'm up for that long of a flight."

"I'll ask them to come here." Kenton closed his eyes and telepathed to Fay. He explained the situation and asked if she and Meena could come right away. If Tally had been on Tarradon, he would have asked her too.

"We'll be there. I'll let Meena know," Fay telepathed back.

"Thank you."

Kenton opened his eyes and gave them his best smile. "My sisters will be here shortly." As if they had been doing nothing, they appeared in the living room. Being able to detect where he was located was an added bonus to being related.

All eyes widened. "Yes, we can teleport. May I present Fay and Meena," Kenton said.

"We met Fay at Birk and Lily's wedding," Tory's mom said.

"Thank you for coming. And so fast."

To her credit, Tory's mom didn't comment on their teleporting abilities, but perhaps Fay had teleported to the wedding.

Fay stepped over to Mr. Sinclair and then looked at everyone else. "If you all wouldn't mind giving us some space?"

"Of course. We'll be in the kitchen." Mrs. Sinclair nodded at Tory, Finn, Greer, and Declan to join her. "I'm going to call Stone and Ramsey. They need to be here," she said as she went toward another room.

Meena looked up at Kenton. "That includes you, brother. We don't need you hovering."

"Fine." He wanted to talk with Tory anyway—or at least find out if she was willing to forgive him for lying to her.

After asking Fay how she planned on healing Tory's father, he went to the kitchen where the five of them were sitting around a table, radiating worry.

Tory motioned he take a seat next to her, and his libido shot skyward. Given the stressful situation, his reaction was totally inappropriate, but he couldn't help himself. Kenton did, however, control his desire to comfort her. He wasn't sure she wanted that at the moment—at least from him.

"Do you think they can help my father?" Tory asked.

"My sister's abilities are extensive. If anyone can help, they can. Usually, they need my third sister for certain spells, but she is stubbornly back home. Don't worry. I'm sure your dad will be fine."

Kenton hoped like hell he hadn't told another lie.

Chapter Sixteen

TORY HADN'T WANTED to need Kenton, but her father's life had been on the line. If neither Greer, Declan, nor his own dragon could help him, her only choice had been to ask Kenton. He'd been able to cure her problems when no one else could, so Tory figured he could do this too. Turns out she had been slightly wrong, but at least Kenton had been kind enough to drag his sisters out late at night to help.

Her mother hung up the phone. "Ramsey and Stone are on their way," her mom said.

"We should call Uncle Laird too," Declan said.

"I will, but I won't ask the Caspians to come over unless Dad's health doesn't improve."

"That might be wise. Too many people might be a bit embarrassing. You know how proud he is," Declan said.

Tory turned to Kenton. "I really appreciate you coming. I know things between us have been...tense."

"I'm happy to help. Anytime." He smiled, and the love in his eyes melted her heart. *Focus, Tory.*

"Was it pure luck that you happened to be at Wings tonight?" She worked hard not to infuse any accusation or any other emotion into her question.

"Honestly? No. I was worried about the demons getting to your family. If I had been in the forest, you might not have been able to find me." He pulled two things out of his pocket and handed her one of them. "Fay made these bracelets for us."

Tory studied the gift. "It's beautiful. I've never seen a stone like this before. What is it?"

"It's a green Orlandan stone. It's found on Feyrion and is very powerful. Put it on, and I'll show you how to use it."

She slipped the bracelet over her wrist, and he put his on. Tory couldn't help but smile. "It fits perfectly."

He nodded. "If you press the stone close to your heart, something special will happen. Try it."

She did as he asked. "Like this?"

"Exactly. It enables us to communicate telepathically without us having fully mated," he telepathed.

Her heart pounded at the words in her head. His lips didn't move, yet she heard everything. "How is this possible?"

"Try communicating with me," he urged.

Once more, the voice came into her head. *"This is remarkable."*

"I know."

"I guess you don't need a cellphone when you can have this." Tory couldn't help but smile.

"With the demon at large and possibly targeting you and your family, I thought you might need my help. I didn't give it to you before, because I didn't want to be so presumptuous to think that you'd want to be in contact with me."

"I'm happy we can contact each other. Is this how people communicate on Feyrion?"

"No. This is special. For us."

Before she could sort out her feelings about this, Fay, Meena, and her dad stepped into the kitchen. Everyone was smiling.

The family rushed up to her father. "Are you okay?" her mom asked.

"Yes, thanks to these wonderful ladies. It was like all of the colors became brighter and the air warmer. I feel better than ever."

"I'm glad we were able to help," Meena said.

"Did you sense a demon had done this?" Tory asked the sisters, wanting to double-check Kenton's theory.

"Yes. Its presence was quite clear."

While she had figured it had been a demon, she was hoping it hadn't been. "It really scares me that I wasn't able to tell it was that Kai person." She shivered.

"At least you know what he looks like," Kenton said. "I hope you will not interact with him in any way from now on."

Kenton's tone had suddenly hardened. "No. I most definitely won't do that." Tory stepped over to Fay and held out her new bracelet. "Thank you for making this for me. It's incredible."

"I was happy to do it. My brother doesn't seem to want to embrace all that Tarradon has to offer, if you know what I mean. I figured you might need to speak with him. Mind you, you can only telepath with Kenton—not with us. And we won't be intruding into your head either." Fay glanced over at her brother. "Sometimes he gets into my head when I'm not in the mood."

From her warm smile, she was kidding.

"I'm sure we will use our communication device effectively and wisely." Tory turned to Kenton. She wasn't ready to totally forgive him, but she was working on it. "Right?"

"Absolutely." He turned to her parents and Finn. "My sisters and I will take our leave. If you need us, you know how to get a hold of us."

"Yes, and thank you again," her dad said.

Tory was tempted to give Kenton a quick kiss, but her head was spinning too much to trust herself.

Without any fanfare, Kenton and his two sisters disappeared. Her mom rushed up to her. "That was amazing that they came so fast and could heal Jamison. It was astounding really." Her mother touched Tory's bracelet. "If Kenton gave you something that enables you two to communicate, something must be going on between you two. Huh? Care to share?"

"Mom," Tory groaned, so not in the mood to spill her guts about Kenton. Even she wasn't totally sure what was happening between them. "It's late."

The front door opened, and a second later, Ramsey and Stone

rushed into the kitchen. "Dad?"

Her father smiled. "I'm fine. Let's head into the living room, and I'll tell you everything." Her father turned to Tory and nodded at Mom. "Be careful with this one," he whispered. "Your mother will make you spill your deepest secrets."

"I'll be careful." She leaned back. "Are you positive you're okay? These demons still scare me to death."

"You and me both. If anyone had asked, I would have said a demon had two heads or maybe more than two eyes. Little did I know they look like us."

"I know, right? I can't believe I was sitting next to one and never suspected anything."

Her dad placed a hand on her shoulder. "I'm just thankful he didn't get into either of our heads."

Wasn't that the truth. "If the only thing these demons can do is make us sick, we're in good shape, though I don't want to have to rely on Fay and Meena each time."

"I agree." Her dad kissed her cheek. "Have a good talk with your mom."

Greer stepped over and hugged her. "I'm going to head out."

"Thanks for coming."

"Anytime. I wish I had been able to help," Greer said.

Declan turned to Mom. "Now that Dad is good, I'm taking off too."

Her mom hugged them both and then clasped Finn's shoulder. "Thank you for bringing Kenton here."

"I was happy to help."

"I will stop over tomorrow to visit with Kaleena and Sapphire. I know she has been worried about her dad," her mom said.

"She'd like that." Finn hugged Mom.

Tory wasn't sure what she was going to say to her mother. Her parents knew that she'd been in Feyrion to heal and for some reason decided not to tell her. But what was past was past. Right now, Tory could use some motherly advice.

Once they were alone, Tory sat at the counter and watched her mother make tea. "I saw the way Kenton looked at you," her mother said.

The slight lift to her mom's lips, along with the way her eyes twinkled, told it all. Even her mom could see the intense attraction, but Tory wanted verbal confirmation "What way is that?"

"Why, Tory Sinclair, you are intuitive, competent, and strong. I can see it in both of your eyes. He's your mate."

Shit. "Kenton claims we are."

"Don't you believe it?"

"I do, but I'm not happy that he didn't tell me that he erased my memory of my time on Feyrion. Even you all kept it from me."

Her mom handed Tory a cup and then picked hers up and sipped it. "You have to understand. We did what we thought was best for you."

Why did everyone think they knew what was best for her? "Are you saying I'm being unfair to him?"

"Perhaps a bit. Maybe there are things in his home world that he didn't want you to see. It might have affected how you treated him going forward. If you two are mates, Kenton would want you to judge him for who he is and not on where he grew up."

Tory hadn't thought of that before. "You might be right."

Her mom set her cup down. "Putting aside the deception, do you like him?"

That was easy to answer. "I find him very attractive. And generous. So yes. I like him. In fact, he's all I think about."

"What's the problem then? Besides the fact he kept something from you."

She inhaled. What was keeping her from embracing this amazing man? "He's powerful."

Her mom's chin tucked in. "Is that a bad thing?"

"He's from another realm."

"So?"

She didn't know why her mother couldn't see the issue. "What if we mate and he suddenly decides he wants us to live on Feyrion?"

"Would it be any different if you'd met someone from Earth? Like Kaleena did."

"Maybe, but bottom line is that Finn moved here."

Her mother placed a hand on Tory's arm. "It's only a portal jump away. Would I be thrilled you might live on another realm? No, but I want you to be happy. If Kenton makes you that way, I say go for it."

"I'm a Guardian. I have duties here."

"And from what everyone has told me, Kenton's job is to guard the portals on Tarradon. Stop analyzing everything."

She could see both sides, which was why she was more frustrated than ever. Tory pushed back her chair with a bit too much force, and it toppled backward. Just as the chair was about to hit the floor, she ran behind it and grabbed the back. She then righted it.

"Tory?" The blood seemed to have drained from her mother's face.

She faced her mom. "I'm sorry. I didn't mean to knock it over."

"I don't care about the chair. I'm talking about how you moved behind the chair in an instant, before it landed. That's not possible."

Yet she had caught it. "I don't remember even doing it." She looked around. "What is going on?"

"It was like you disappeared for a second and then appeared someplace else."

She chuckled, probably because what she was about to say sounded impossible. "So I can teleport now just because I slept with Kenton one time?" Oh, crap, crap, crap. That just flew out of her mouth.

Her mom smiled. "You do like him. I knew it."

Tory rarely found a man exciting enough—or trustworthy enough—to sleep with. "Yes, but that doesn't explain my speed, though it has happened a few times already. I brushed it off to fast reflexes."

Her mom sat up straighter. "Try teleporting to the living room."

"I can't teleport, Mom."

"You couldn't before, but maybe you can now. Just try it. For me."

Tory thought it best to humor her mother, but no matter how much Tory pictured moving from one place to another, nothing happened. "See? I can't."

"I would ask Kenton about it."

"I don't want him to think I'm a wannabe Fey or anything. If something like this happens again, I might question him."

"You do that, dear."

Tory had a feeling that the life light Kenton put inside her might be affecting her, but surely it couldn't turn her into a Fey, could it?

"THANK YOU AGAIN for helping out," Kenton told both of his sisters once they were back home.

"I'm glad we were able to help him, but I'm not sure we will be able to a second time," Meena said.

He didn't like the sound of that. "Why?"

"Sometimes spells lose their effectiveness the second time around. The darkness inside him wasn't anything I've dealt with before. Without Fay's help, I'm not sure I could have cured him."

That wasn't good. "I'll be sure to warn them. The scariest part is that Mr. Sinclair didn't sense the demon. From what we know, the Guardians can detect a lot of things."

"They never knew Malpan was a dark Fey."

"True." All the more reason Kenton needed to protect Tory.

Kenton hugged them each—something he rarely did—and then returned to his house where he found Bevon lounging on the sofa. "Welcome back, brother," Kenton said.

"Thanks."

"How did your trip go?" Kenton asked.

"Good. I had a nice chat with Mom."

Kenton pulled a much-needed beer from the refrigerator and then sat in the living room, ready to give Bevon his undivided attention. "Tell me."

"Apparently, these Gromleys used to live on Feyrion outside of the Royal realm."

Kenton had no idea they had been anywhere on his home world. "Don't tell me someone saw fit to boot them out, too?"

"Then I won't tell you, but spoiler alert—we did."

Damn. "They must have done something terrible to be evicted."

Bevon tossed back his beer. "As a matter of fact, their little secret was discovered about six hundred years ago."

"Before they arrived on Tarradon."

"Apparently."

"What was this secret?" Kenton asked.

"Back then, many of the Gromleys were sterile. Before you ask how they could still be around with such a problem, the little buggers figured out a way to circumvent this issue."

In need of a small distraction, Kenton chugged most of his beer. Clearly, his brother was enjoying the telling of his findings in bits and pieces. "What was their solution?" Kenton asked.

"They stole souls of the humans who were either severely injured or dying and then implanted that soul in themselves. That added bit of human altered their anatomy just enough to allow them to reproduce."

That was sick. "Out of curiosity, would all of the humans have died anyway?" Kenton asked.

"We have no way of knowing, but odds are, some would have survived. The Gromleys didn't give them the chance to heal."

Kenton studied his brother to make sure Bevon wasn't making this up. The horror of it all made him sick to his stomach. "I can see why we booted them out."

Bevon stretched an arm across the back of the sofa. "Me, too. Just so you don't think I'm a cold-hearted person, I didn't return here right away because it took me a day or two to process it all. I mean, this is a total nightmare."

Kenton rested his elbows on his knees and dangled the beer bottle between his legs. "Remind me not to wish for that talent. Ever. This means they are very powerful." He blew out a breath. "Do you think the Feys or the Fairies expelled them from Feyrion to Tarradon, where they continued their reign of terror?"

"That would be my guess. Who else besides our kind has that much magic?"

"No one." Kenton told Bevon what Logan had found out about the five victims, and how they were related to those who kicked out the Gromleys from Tarradon. "What I don't get is why come back hundreds of years later?" Kenton asked.

"Who knows? Something must have triggered it. They might think of themselves as victims, but they did kill five people."

"I agree. These newcomers possess the ability to control minds and are, maybe, stealing souls once more."

"I'm thinking we'll never know if the demons took any souls this time, but you said those who died were not ill. That means this isn't the same as what happened before."

"They weren't ill, so this might be just for revenge and not have anything to do with reproduction," Kenton said.

Bevon shook his head. "Part of me wants to meet this person so I can rip out his heart. The other part wants to avoid him. That, however, is not a viable option."

Kenton huffed. "Agreed. One of them already tried to harm Tory's father. Thankfully, he failed since Guardians possess enough magic to thwart his mind-altering abilities."

Bevon sat up and set his beer on the coffee table. "Tory's father was attacked? Is he okay?"

"He is now, but we believe he was merely touched. I was unable to help him, so I had to call on Fay and Meena. They succeeded in drawing out the demon darkness."

"Is that where you've been tonight, trying to cure him?"

"Yes."

Bevon tapped his fingers on his bottle. "Do you have a plan on how to stop these monsters? We need to eradicate them before they harm anyone else."

"I agree, but no, I don't have a plan yet," Kenton said.

"Was Logan able to find anyone else who might be related to the original evictors?"

"Not that I know of, but if he does learn of who else might be related to these old families, I trust the Avonbelle Province Police will do their best to protect them."

"When will you speak with Tory next? I hope she will warn her family about these monsters."

"She already has, but I'll see her tomorrow. She seemed less upset with me after I helped save her father. I'm hoping I can convince her to go to Feyrion with me so she will be safe."

Bevon whistled. "Do you think she is ready for that?"

"She will have to be ready at some point. I want to show her that Feyrion isn't a scary place. Plus, it will give you a chance to find this demon while we are safe and sound."

"Me?"

Bevon was only kidding. He loved challenges. "Yes. I can send a few helpers back if you want."

"That might be a good idea."

"Great. When I approach Tory, I'll suggest we only stay for a day or two. It will be just long enough to show her how amazing our realm is."

Bevon picked up his near empty bottle and saluted. "Good luck."

"I'll need it."

Chapter Seventeen

"I STILL CAN'T believe you kept Kenton's secret from me all this time," Tory said the next morning at work.

Greer held up her hands. "Trust me. It was one of the hardest things I've ever had to do. If I'd known you two were mates, I would have marched my butt to the eternal flame and demand he come clean. Relationships need honesty."

Tory laughed. "I can so see you doing that, but he was partially right in withholding the information for as long as he did. I wasn't ready to learn that I'd almost died. I might have had a setback or something if I woke up in another realm."

"True. If we had told you the moment you woke up that Griffin allowed some stranger to take you to Feyrion—a place we had no idea how to reach—how would you have treated my brother?"

She blew out a breath. "I don't know. I probably would have told him that he had been too reckless with my life." Tory sighed. "Fine. I guess you all were right. In the end, it worked out well."

Greer smiled. "Speaking of turning out well, lookie who is walking across the street right as we speak."

Tory turned and spotted Kenton. Her heart pulsed hot as excitement slid up her body. Somehow her anger toward him must have melted away after he'd saved her dad last night. It hadn't hurt that her mom helped clear up a few of her pressing concerns.

Greer buzzed Kenton in. "Hi, ladies."

"Kenton. You're looking spiffy today," Greer said. "I like the shirt."

"Thank you. I went shopping. Bevon, as well as my sisters, kept telling me that harem pants—if that is what they are called—are not in style here, nor was my peasant shirt."

"Jeans are a better look," Tory shamelessly chimed in as she checked him out.

"Can I talk with you for a moment?" Kenton asked her.

"Sure. How about we step into the back room?"

Greer chuckled. "Take your time."

I'm sensing a make-out session, her dragon said with a lot of glee.

Cool your jets. I imagine he is here about information on the demon.

Tory and Kenton had just reached the backroom when another customer rang the doorbell. The door clicked, and Kenton stiffened. Tory spun around to see what had caused his reaction. Uh-oh. "That's Kai. Can you sense if he is a demon?"

"I can, and he is. Stay here," he commanded.

Tory wanted to follow him out but considering Kai might have been the one to make her dad sick, it would be better if she remained hidden. The problem was that Greer was out there. If this demon touched her cousin, he could infect her too.

"Sir, I'm the new manager here. Can I help you? Greer, you're needed in the back room."

"Sure." A second later the door to the back room opened. "What the hell is Kenton doing?" her cousin asked.

Tory didn't know whether to be mad, scared, or upset. "Kenton has reason to believe that man is the demon who infected my Dad."

She said nothing for a moment. "How could he tell?"

"You didn't sense something was different about him?" Greer was very intuitive.

"I thought I did, but then I dismissed it. It wasn't like anything I've felt before though."

"Did you feel evil?"

Greer bit down on her bottom lip. "It was more anger than anything."

The door clicked shut, and Kenton returned. "All clear, ladies."

"What did you tell Kai?" Tory asked.

"When he told me he wanted to speak with you, I told him that I was your fiancé and that I didn't like you speaking with other men." He held up a hand. "It was a story I had to tell. He didn't seem to be interested in Greer."

Tory blew out a breath. "Did he say he wasn't interested in Greer?"

"No, but he might not have known Greer was related to you."

As much as Tory wanted to pretend this would all go away, she couldn't. "Do you know how we can kill him?"

Kenton dragged a hand down her hair and then cupped her cheek. "My brave warrior. You can't do anything—at least not right now. We have something on Feyrion that might be able to stop him. Would you be willing to take a day or two and help me find this magic ball?"

Tory did want to go, partly to see what was on Feyrion, and partly because she wanted to give their relationship a second chance. She looked over at Greer. "The next two days are your days off."

"It's okay," Greer said. "This is important, so go. You covered for me when that dark entity had captured me."

"Thank you. I probably won't be able to contact you during that time."

Greer smiled. "You'll be safe with Kenton." Greer hugged her.

"Ready?" he asked.

"I'll need to pick up a few things from home."

"Understood." Kenton placed a hand on her back, and before she could blink, they were standing in her living room. "Pack light."

"I'm not sure I'll ever get used to this teleporting stuff."

He smiled. "When you do, you'll never want to fly again."

She loved soaring through the air. The cool wind against her skin invigorated her. "Give me a sec. You'll be here when I return, right?"

He grinned. "I'll never leave you again like that. I promise."

"Okay. I'll be right back."

Tory threw some essentials into a backpack purse, so that she wouldn't have to carry it far when they arrived. Knowing Kenton though, he'd teleport them to their hotel room—or wherever he used to live. Dang. She knew almost nothing about him. If they were to be mates, she needed to find out more.

Knowing her family would worry if they tried to contact her and she didn't answer, Tory called her mom.

"Hi, dear. Is everything okay?"

Her mother was quite intuitive also. "Kenton and I are going to Feyrion for a couple of days. We want to see if we can figure out how to kill a demon."

"Oh, Tory. Are you sure it will be safe?"

"I'll be safer on Feyrion than on Tarradon."

Her mother said nothing for a moment. "Thanks for letting me know. I'll tell the others we might have a solution to our problem."

"Thanks, Mom. I love you."

"Love you too."

Tory went back to the living room where Kenton was thankfully waiting for her. "We'll need to teleport to my cabin in the woods. From there, we'll go through the portal," he said. "I could create a portal from here, but it wouldn't be as secure as the one in the woods. With the demons at large, I don't want to risk it. It will only take us a few seconds."

"Works for me."

True to his word, they arrived in his house in seconds. She looked around. While the space wasn't overly large, neither was her house. It actually had a similar layout to her place. "It's very rustic."

"Not your taste, I see, but I can change it quite easily. However, we can decorate later. We should get to Feyrion."

"Of course." Tory wasn't sure where the portal was, but she really didn't need to know.

He led her down a long hallway toward a door and then opened it. Once second, she was standing on the hardwood floors of his cabin, and the next, she was in front of a palace or maybe she'd call it a castle. It was built from beautiful white stone and had two towers that bordered the front entrance. It was huge. Colorful flowers abounded everywhere—in front of the castle as well as in the surrounding fields. She inhaled. "This place smells amazing."

Kenton smiled. "The colors are brighter, the sounds clearer, the smells more intense. Everything is heightened here. With your ability to see and hear better than regular humans, this might be overwhelming at first, but you'll get used to it."

"The warmth, sunlight, and beauty is really calming."

He grinned. "Come on. It's time to meet the rest of the family."

When he placed a hand on her back and led her forward, Tory stopped. "You live here?" This was a far cry from his cabin.

"Actually, my parents live here. Did I forget to tell you they are the king and queen of Feyrion?"

OKAY, KENTON PROBABLY could have handled that better, but if he had told Tory he was royalty from the start, she might have balked. The royalty on Tarradon were enemies to the Guardians. It didn't matter she'd told him that her mother was the queen's sister. In that respect, Tory was practically royalty too. Possibly, he didn't tell her because Kenton didn't want her to want him just because of the riches and power that were at his command—or would be once the king and queen decided they'd had enough.

"Yes, you forgot to mention that little fact," Tory said. "You really should do something about your poor memory, you know."

Thankfully, she smiled after that comment. "I will take that under advisement. Before we go in, I'll give you a little background. My parents are nice, or rather my mother who is a Fairy, is very gentle and caring. My dad is Fey. As the king, he has to be a bit more aggressive. He might not show his emotions very often, but he is a good man."

She touched his arm. "As are you."

"Thank you. I try to be."

Kenton could have teleported directly into the living room, but he wanted her to experience everything, so he walked her up the driveway to the entrance, and then escorted her inside. While the outside was large and grand, the inside was rather understated. There might be many masterpieces on the walls, but the surface was coated in regular paint like everyone else's home. The furniture was more upscale than that of a typical family's home, but all of the statues were made by locals.

"This is amazing," she said with awe.

Marnia, one of their maids, came down the hallway carrying a broom. Kenton stopped her. "Mr. Kenton. Welcome home." She glanced over at Tory and then shifted her gaze downward.

"Marnia, this is my friend, Tory." He wasn't sure if he should announce that Tory was his mate just yet.

"Ma'am."

"Do you know where Mother is?"

"She is in the kitchen."

"Thank you, Marnia."

Kenton led Tory toward the back of the castle. "Your mother cooks?" she asked.

He laughed. "I would say she snacks on what others are making more than she actually cooks, though she is a rather competent chef."

Inside the too warm kitchen, his mom was conversing with their master chef. She was wearing a rather tattered apron, her hair was pulled back into a ponytail with wisps all over the place, and she had flour on her hands.

"Mother?"

She looked over and grinned. "Kenton! This is a surprise."

She wiped her hands on a nearby towel and then rushed over to him. He caught her quick glance at Tory.

"Mom, you remember Tory."

"Of course. I'm glad to see you looking so healthy. That terrible dark Fey did quite a number on you."

"Tory, this is my mother, Queen Arianna."

"It is a pleasure to meet you, Queen Arianna. I suppose Malpan did harm me, but I honestly remember nothing."

"Yes, that was my idea. Before I was sure you and Kenton were mates, I had no choice but to make certain you didn't return to Tarradon telling tales. We try to keep our perfect little realm all to ourselves."

He didn't need his mother to say anything else that would embarrass him. *"Can we talk for a moment?"* he telepathed.

"Of course, dear."

"How about the drawing room?"

"Let me wash my hands, and I'll meet you there." His mom clasped his hand. *"How are things going between you two?"*

Tory would become uncomfortable if he and his mom stood there in silence for long. *"Good, but the lies have put a strain on things."*

She smiled, clearly pretending the two of them hadn't been discussing Tory.

Kenton turned his attention back to his mate. "We'll meet mom in the drawing room once she cleans up. Come this way."

Once they were seated, he asked what Tory wanted to drink.

"Do you have the same drinks as on Tarradon?"

"Not exactly, though we do have coffee and tea. No soda though." He leaned forward. "We borrowed a few sprigs of your coffee plants so we could grow it here."

Her eyebrows rose. "Is that so? Don't worry. I won't tell. I think we did the same when we visited Earth."

Kenton smiled, thrilled that Tory could be relaxed when everything around her was so new.

Queen Arianna breezed into the room. She'd changed and cleaned up. Her hair was now in a twisted updo, and she wore a beautiful purple flowing gown with gold inter-woven around the edges. Tory's mouth opened, probably because it had only been a minute or two since his mother had left to change.

His mom sat in one of the high-backed chairs across from them.

"Tea or coffee?" she asked.

"How about iced tea?" Tory asked.

His mom swept a hand across the table and the tea appeared. "And for you, Kenton?"

"The same. Thank you, Mother." Though he'd rather have a beer. As kind and wonderful as his mother was, it often was stressful being home, especially when she brought up the topic of whether he was ready to take over running the realm.

"Please don't mention anything about the politics of the realm, Mom," he telepathed. *"Tory isn't ready yet."*

"I'm not insensitive." She turned to Tory. "Tell me about yourself, dear."

That might be just as bad. His mate didn't need to be grilled by his mother, but he supposed that kind of thing happened on Tarradon too. For the next half hour, Tory discussed her job at the store. To his delight, she told his mom that everyone in her family was a Guardian."

"That's wonderful. We're kind of Guardians too. We protect what we have here. Kenton is in charge of our military—if that is what they are called."

"Mother." He needed to get to the point of their visit. "I'm sure Bevon explained about the current issue on Tarradon."

"You mean the demons?"

"Yes. Do you think you could give us a hand in creating a magic ball of light to destroy them?"

"I can, but your three sisters can perform the spell just as well, assuming I give them a bit of my special magic."

"Then we need to speak with Tally. She'll have to return with us, if only for a little while."

His mom pressed her lips together. "I'll see what I can do. In the meantime, why don't you show Tory what Feyrion has to offer. I'll let you know if I'm successful."

He stood. "Thank you." He faced Tory. "Ready?"

Her mouth opened and then closed. "Sure."

Kenton took her hand and teleported them to one of his favorite spots.

"Whoa." Tory looked around. "This is incredible."

"I never get tired of looking at the tall mountains, the thick green frenlen trees, and the crystalline water of the lake below."

She inhaled. "It smells sweet. It's like the air is totally pure."

"It is."

Tory faced him. "Why would you leave here? It seems idyllic."

"The operative word is *seems*. How about we go for a swim, and I'll tell you all about it?"

"I didn't bring a bathing suit."

He hadn't expected her to have that objection. "I can put a cloaking spell around us so no one can see us. I swim in the nude in case you're wondering." Her eyes widened. "Don't look so shocked. It's not like you haven't seen my junk before."

She cracked up. "You call it junk here, too?"

Kenton never wanted to lie to her again. "No. I picked up that slang expression while working at Angelique's Coffee Shop."

"Seriously?"

He nodded. "You'd be surprised what people talk about when they don't think anyone is listening. Let's go."

One second, they were standing on top of the mountain, and the next they were at the bottom of the mountain range, feet half sunken on the white sand beach.

"Teleporting is still a thrill. I'm not sure I'll get used to it."

"You will. Come on. The water is warm. I can turn my back while you undress if you'd feel more comfortable."

"Funny man. Why don't you do that hand swiping thing and remove both of our clothes at the same time?"

"It would be my pleasure, just as soon as I cloak this area."

Chapter Eighteen

TORY INSTANTLY COVERED herself—not from Kenton but from anyone who might be watching.

He laughed. "No one can see you."

She looked around. "Are you sure your shield is up?"

"Yes, I'll show you." He swept his hand, wiggling his fingers in some odd pattern. As quickly as her clothes disappeared, they reappeared. "Walk up the beach a bit and then turn around. If you want, you can use your bracelet to communicate telepathically with me."

This was beyond cool. Dragons had powers but nothing like this. To test out the bracelet, she swiveled the band around so that the stone was over her inner wrist, and then she placed it over her heart. Tory then walked down the beach. *"Tell me when I can turn around,"* she telepathed.

"Now is good."

She spun around and stilled. The beach, water, and hills were still there but not Kenton. "Where are you?"

He chuckled. *"Right where you left me."*

"Can you see me?" she asked.

"Yes. You are outside this small sphere I have created."

"That is incredible."

Tory headed back to where she believed him to be. As if she'd stepped through a portal, there he was! "That was almost scary but cool at the same time."

Kenton stepped up to her. "Is that so?" He cocked a brow. "I have a few other tricks I can show you."

Tory grinned. "I can't wait."

With another sweep of his hand, she was naked—except for her bracelet. She liked that he kept it on her. To her delight their clothes lay in a neat pile on the sand.

He held out his hand. "Let's check out the water."

"Is it cold?"

"No. It's perfect, assuming I guessed the temperature you like."

She stopped. "Don't tell me, you can change water temperature with a sweep of a hand too?"

"I can do a lot of things."

The water was an incredibly beautiful aquamarine blue that shimmered when the sun's rays bounced off the surface. Tory had never seen anything quite like it. Kenton led her into the water. True to his word, it was perfect. Not bathwater warm but not chilly either. When they were waist height, she expected him to kiss her. Instead, he dove under the surface and swam toward the middle of the lake as fast as any dolphin could. Tory was tempted to shift into her dragon form and chase after him.

I'm game, her dragon said.

If Kenton could show off, she could too! It was a little tricky shifting since she was partially submerged already, but once she did, Tory dove down. The problem was that the lake was a bit shallow for her large body, but once she became horizontal, she moved forward quickly. Once she was close to the middle of the lake, she became fully submerged and only had to wag her tail twice to reach him. She surfaced and then shifted back into her human form.

Kenton clapped while treading water. "Show off."

She laughed. "You inspired me."

He clasped her waist, and when he pulled her close, she then wrapped her legs around his waist.

"It's you who inspire me," Kenton said, his eyes the color of pure gold.

A moment later, they were on the opposite end of the lake where Kenton could stand. "A girl could get used to this teleporting thing."

"You will have that ability soon."

Her heart pumped hard. He meant after they mated. "I hope so."

She wasn't ready to discuss that step right now, not when all she could focus on were his delicious lips. Tory leaned in and kissed him, and it was as if sunshine and warmth filled her. Even her heart heated up, if that was even possible. When their tongues touched, the sensations intensified. Her pulse soared as need grabbed her so hard, she felt as if she might burst. While the last time they'd made love had been monumental, this was different—more surreal perhaps.

Kenton dragged his hands down her body, lighting her up along the way. "How about we get more comfortable?"

With him, anything was possible. "What do you have in mind?"

In a blink of an eye, they were in a forest. Light was streaming through the leaves, and a small clear river was gurgling alongside them. With a sweep of a hand, a blanket appeared that was spread out on the ground. Without a word, he knelt, and Tory's feet hit the ground. With a quick flip, she was on her back with Kenton on top. Convinced the world only existed except for them, they kissed and touched, all the while moaning and groaning. When Kenton slipped down and nabbed a nipple between his teeth, her scales flashed brighter than ever. Out of the corner of her eye, a glow pulsed around her heart. Was that where he'd implanted his life light?

"Yes!" she nearly shouted when he fingered her, making her temporarily forget about her newfound light.

His ability to find that perfect spot inside her that triggered all of her desires was truly magical. He pressed, twisted, and swept his finger until her climax built so fast she was unable to stop it.

Tory grabbed his shoulders and held on for dear life as her orgasm swept through her with force. Her body collapsed as she let out a large breath. As much as she would have enjoyed not moving for a while, when he slipped lower, she tightened her grip on his shoulders.

"My turn," she whispered.

He looked up. "To do what?"

Surely, he wasn't that clueless. "Before you perform your amazing tongue dance between my legs, I want to return the favor. If I recall, you stopped me the last time."

Kenton rolled onto his back. "Fair is fair, love."

Tory rose to her knees and scanned his body. Oh, my. She wanted to touch, kiss, and taste every inch of him. Between the gurgling water, the gentle breeze, and the rustling of leaves, she'd never been this calm or this excited. The combination sent erotic pulses up and down her body.

His light was doing a dance in his chest, flashing at random intervals. Tory placed a palm over his heart and instantly felt his heat and, dare she say, love. "I can almost feel the connection."

He reached up and stroked her head. "We are connected in the deepest and most intimate way. We're mates. Forever. We will eventually share our mutual talents when you are ready."

Tory had to work hard not to swoon at his words. While she wanted to tell him she was almost ready to mate, the words refused to form. Instead, she turned her attention to his twitching cock that she was sure he was moving.

"Back to the task at hand. Or rather mouth." Tory laughed at her own joke.

She leaned over, grabbed his cock and squeezed it, loving its length, girth, and the strength pouring out of it. When she pumped her fist, Kenton closed his eyes and inhaled fully while digging his nails into the blanket. The fact he was this receptive spurred her on.

While she wanted to tempt and tease him until he came, she needed him too much for prolonged contact. It was almost as if being on Feyrion made her desires go haywire. Keeping her hand on his dick, she drew him deep into her mouth.

"Holy goddess," he ground out.

Thrilled she excited him as much as he turned her on, she swirled her tongue around the length and then lifted off of him. His eyes opened, and he clasped her wrist. Tory almost laughed. She'd had a kitten once who never wanted Tory to stop petting her. Kenton seemed to be the same.

Continuing her sensual assault, she licked the rim of his cock before sucking on it again. When she tasted a bit of cum, she pulled off. Tory had planned to ride him, but Kenton seemed to have something else in mind, because he had her back underneath him in a flash with his thick dick at her entrance.

"Drat," he said as he dropped to the side. "Condom."

Tory would have to get some kind of protection now that Kenton was in her life. He did his finger waving thing, and a condom appeared in his grasp. As if he could make it teleport, he was covered before she could blink.

He smiled. "Now, where were we?"

"I'm sure you can figure it out."

Kenton leaned over and kissed her. Tenderness poured out of him as he slid right into her, filling her to the max. Something was happening to her. What exactly it was, she wasn't sure other than she loved this intense feeling of euphoria.

Their tongues sparred and explored. Tory threaded her arms under his, and when she dragged her too sharp nails down his back, his muscles bunched and flexed. Kenton Forrester might be a Fey, but he was definitely all man. Only now, he was her man.

He broke the kiss, slid his hands down to her waist, and then dragged his mouth to that sensitive spot right below her ear. "I need you, Tory Sinclair, more than you can know."

His words should have scared her, but they didn't. Knowing how much he cared urged her to take what she wanted, but as tempted as Tory was to mate with him, it wasn't the time. A small part of her still harbored some resentment over the lies, wondering if there would be more.

When he tugged on her earlobe, she forgot about her anger and seized the moment. She slid her hands down to his thrusting hips and grabbed his ass. Tory held on tight for this rollercoaster of a ride.

Needing to kiss him, she turned her head. His gaze locked onto hers, and he devoured her with enough lust and passion to change her soul. Tory planted her feet on the blanket and pressed upward. The ensuing loving was fast, furious, and oh so delicious, causing parts of her body that she never knew existed to come alive. When he gently bit down on her lower lip and grunted, Tory came so hard, she thought her heart would stop.

"Tory, my queen," Kenton whispered.

Two thrusts later, he came too. He then slipped his hands under her and rolled them over. Emotionally spent, she lowered her cheek onto his chest and closed her eyes.

When she awoke, they were back on the beach at the base of the mountain. She looked around, and her palm went to her chest. "I will not get used to teleporting. A little warning next time?"

Kenton laughed. "I promise. Let's take a dip and wash up."

The water that had been rather warm was now cool. She looked up at him. "Did you change the temperature or something? Or am I just hot?"

"That's a loaded question. You are very hot, but yes, I changed the water temperature. I thought after our heated exercise that you'd enjoy the change."

Wow. "Is there anything you can't do?"

"Too much, I'm afraid. You've already witnessed a few of my faults."

Was he referring to withholding information? "I've detected none." Why spoil a perfectly good day?

For the next few minutes, they swam, challenged each other, and just played in the water.

"Ready to head back to reality?" he asked.

"Where exactly is that?" She didn't know if he planned to create a portal back to Tarradon or have them stay on Feyrion.

He cupped her face. "First, we should go to the beach. While I could dress you here, I don't think it would be pleasant wearing wet clothes. Then we'll head back to my parents' home."

He had a point. "Okay."

In less than a breath's time, they were dry and dressed. Someday, this might be commonplace but not in the near future.

"Now let's head back to the castle. I want to see if my mother made any progress in getting Tally to help create the magic ball. I also told Bevon I would round up a few men to help with the demon issue. I'm not quite sure what they can do against one if they don't have the magic ball, but I imagine they can slow him down."

Tory ran a hand down his arm. "Thank you. I know this isn't your fight."

"Oh, but it is. Actually, it is our fault." He explained how the Gromleys were on Feyrion first. "They did unspeakable things to our people, so we tossed them out."

"To Tarradon?"

His lips pulled back. "I'm afraid so. I was not involved. Trust me. The Tarradonians eventually kicked the Gromleys out and sent them to Cargonia. Just think how pissed the Cargonians must have been."

Kenton made sense. "Okay, so we are all complicit in this misadventure."

He smiled. "Come on. I'll round up a few men, and then we can head back to Tarradon after I speak with my folks."

They'd only arrived in his land a few hours ago. She thought they would be staying a few days. Maybe Kenton needed to guard the portals. Who was she to suggest they stay? "Do you think some demons will try to come to Feyrion to exact revenge?"

He tapped her nose. "They might try, but they wouldn't be successful. It was why I wanted to come here, so you'd be safe for at least one day. I also wanted to show you that Feyrion is an amazing place."

"It's a fairyland."

"The area surrounding the royal realm is indeed wonderful, but there are parts of this realm that could use some taming."

"I think every realm could say that."

Kenton placed a hand on her back. "I agree."

This time when they arrived—or should she say popped up—
Tory wasn't as shocked about the abrupt change of location. He took
them to the drawing room of the castle.

"Now all we need is to convince Tally to help."

Chapter Nineteen

ALL IN ALL, Kenton thought this little trip to Feyrion was a success, in large part because Tory and his mom seemed to get along really well. In a way, he was thankful his father had not been in town, because it gave Tory and him time to have that fantastic interlude in the forest and playtime in the lake. That lovemaking had been even more spectacular than the first time.

"Tally will help with the magic ball?" he asked his mother.

"Yes, but I need to locate the spell book," his mother said. "Go help Bevon in case the demon returns. I'll let you know when we have the ball."

"Thanks."

Not wanting to overwhelm Tory on her first time to his homeland, it was time to leave. No telling if this environment would trigger any of the magic inside her, but he needed to warn her in case it did.

"Ready to go?" he asked.

"Yes." Tory faced Queen Arianna and held out a hand. "Thank you for making me feel welcome."

"Anytime, my sweet girl." His mom smiled, opened her arms, and hugged his mate.

As happy as he was that his mother had so warmly welcomed her, Kenton could only imagine the strife that was about to happen when Tory learned of his final lie.

He placed a hand on her back to connect them and teleported to the portal that led to Tarradon. He swept his hand around in a large arc and said the passwords required to open the portal. Once it appeared, they both stepped through.

When entering Feyrion, the portal sat behind their homes. When arriving, it opened up in front. They stepped foot in the forest and froze.

She grabbed his arm. "Kai?" Tory asked. "What are you doing here?"

Sure as shit, the demon was standing there with a stupid grin on his face. Kenton's blood pressure rose—something rare for a Fey. He looked around for Bevon, hoping for a little backup. Either his brother was off doing something, or he was in the house, unaware of anything.

"I've come to see you both," Kai said.

The demon stepped toward them, and Kenton returned his attention to the threat. "How did you find us?"

"People talk."

Now wasn't the time to extract names. "What do you really want, Kai?"

"You know."

Kenton placed a hand over his bracelet, hoping to communicate with Tory. *Tory, go inside.*

She didn't answer right away. *Okay.*

He had to admit, he hadn't expected her to give in so easily, but he was happy she did.

Bevon, we could use a little help, Kenton telepathed.

In the middle of something, brother, Bevon responded. *Be there in a jiff.*

It's nothing critical. Thanks for asking. It's just a demon outside our home.

Crap. I'm with the two men you sent as we speak.

The front door to his house clicked closed. "Talk to you in a bit, Tory," Kai shouted and then smiled.

Bastard. Kai was probably happy Kenton's fire shooting mate had gone inside, though the demon might like the heat since he glowed when angered.

The best approach was to make the demon believe that Kenton sympathized with his plight. He did in a way, but there had been a good reason why the man's family had been banned in the first place. They were murderers.

Kenton crossed his arms over his chest. "You slit the throats of five innocent people. Why?"

Kai's eyes widened. "I'm impressed you figured it out."

"It's not as if your kind are new to the Feys. I'm curious what their deaths accomplished." Kenton suspected the answer, but he wanted confirmation.

"I wanted revenge for what happened here."

Kenton's stomach churned, but he forced down the anger. It didn't matter Bevon had already told him this before. "Why those five?"

"Their ancient family members were the ones who harmed my family."

Logan's investigation had been correct. "I'm betting none of them had even heard of your family."

"It doesn't matter. Their deaths helped draw you out. You Feys are hard to find."

"A phone call would have sufficed." Not that he even had a phone. Bevon did, but he doubted many had his number.

The demon smiled. "My way is better."

"Why come to me?"

"I want your family to suffer like mine did, which is why I plan to kill you."

Kenton wasn't about to admit that he couldn't be killed—except if he ingested Treniam.

"My family?" Sure, he was stalling, but he was waiting for Bevon to arrive so his brother could protect Tory while Kenton dealt with this idiot.

"The same thing happened on Feyrion. Did you know that was where my family came from?"

"Interesting," he said with as much calm as possible. He felt no need to admit he knew the Gromleys were from there. "Before you attempt to take my life, answer me one more thing. Did it make you feel better when you forced those five people to slit their throats?"

"Why yes it did." Kai's chin lifted. "I could almost hear my ancestors cheering."

Kenton had to swallow his disgust. "How many other demons are with you on Tarradon?" He was quite sure none had breached the portal to Feyrion.

Kai smiled. "Wouldn't you like to know?"

Yes, he would. "Will killing me make up for what those in my realm did to your family?"

"It will to me." The demon slipped a hand in his pocket and pulled out what looked like a bunch of herbs—Treniam to be exact. That was impossible since the plant only grew on Feyrion.

"Where did you get that?" Kenton's voice wavered, and Kai grinned. Drat. The demon couldn't have gone to his homeland. The royal guards would have stopped him.

"Oh, this little old stuff? Right before your people expelled us from Feyrion, we grabbed a few plants. We grew a crop right here on Tarradon. You'd be surprised how well it has prospered in the Tarradonian soil."

Shit. Shit. Shit. "What good will it do you?" His voice might have been the epitome of calm, but his gut was churning up a storm.

"I heard if it even touches your skin that it will weaken you."

While true, Kenton wasn't about to admit it. "You are misinformed."

"Then you won't mind if I try it."

The teleporting demon was on Kenton in a flash. Before Kenton could stop him, fire burned his skin. Withstanding the pain wasn't the issue. It was that the poison sinking into his skin was causing the harm.

His mind fuzzed. *"Bevon,"* he telepathed. Kenton dropped to his knees before he could finish communicating with his brother.

For no apparent reason, the demon flew backward, slammed

against a tree, and landed with a thud.

Gentle hands grabbed Kenton's shoulders. "Kenton, are you okay?"

"Tory?" What was she doing there? Hadn't he told her to stay put?

Bevon and two other Feys appeared and faced Kai, arms crossed. "Leave and don't come back," Bevon commanded.

One second later, the demon was gone. The fuss that followed was totally embarrassing. Kenton had never been this incapacitated before. "I'm okay," he managed to say, though from the way he was panting, he clearly was not.

"No, you aren't," Tory said.

"She's right, brother. Can you teleport into the house?" Bevon telepathed.

If he couldn't do that, he'd be completely devastated. Thankfully, both he and Tory instantly returned to the bedroom since she'd been touching him at the time.

Her hands shook, and her legs seemed less than steady when she stood up from the bed and faced him.

"Are you okay?" he asked.

"Me? Yes and no."

Before he could ask her what was troubling her, Fay, Meena, and Bevon were by his side. "Treniam? How the hell did he get a hold of that?" Bevon asked.

"He said centuries ago when his family was banished from Feyrion, they removed a bunch of it and began growing it somewhere on Tarradon."

"Thank goodness you didn't ingest any. You might have died," Fay said with too much concern.

"You don't need to remind me."

"Let us heal you," Meena said.

While he didn't like Tory to see him in this condition, she needed to understand everything about being Fey. "Be quick about it."

Fay glanced to the ceiling and shook her head slightly. She then cupped his face while Meena scooted onto the bed next to him and clasped both of his arms. Together they chanted something in ancient Feyrionian while both Tory and Bevon watched. Slowly, the poison leached out of his body. When they let go, relief washed through him.

Kenton smiled. "Thank you. Your powers have come in handy more times than I can count." He hugged each of them.

"Stay away from that demon," Fay warned.

"Yes, sister." Both were bossy, but Fay was more so.

They disappeared.

"I'm going to talk to the men," Bevon said. "We need to find the source of the Treniam and destroy it."

Kenton—and any other royal—was quite powerless against a demon who possessed that plant. "That would be wise."

When Bevon disappeared, Kenton turned back to his mate. Tory was sitting across the room on a chair. She looked anything but fine. Kenton walked over to her, knelt in front of her, and clasped her hands. "Tell me what's wrong. I'm better, by the way."

"I know, but I can't stop thinking about what happened out there."

"Yes, a demon tried to kill me. I was there."

"I was talking about how that demon flew through the air."

He too was a bit confused how that had happened. "Did one of my sisters or Bevon do that?" His heart pumped hard. Or were Tory's powers finally coming through?

"No. I think I did it. I wanted to see what was happening out-side, so I stepped onto the porch. Without warning, Kai was on you in a flash. When I saw you fall, I just held out my hands and yelled at him to stop. That was all. Next thing I knew, he was thrown backward."

Only now did he remember her calling out. It had to have been her powers kicking in. Neither Bevon nor the other two men had arrived yet, and Fay and Meena would have told him if they'd helped. He had to tell Tory she'd been responsible. She was bound to find out soon enough. Kenton sat on his haunches. "I'll tell you what I think happened, but please do not get upset."

She stilled. "Upset?"

"I know you're going to say I should have warned you sooner, but you weren't ready."

"Ready for what?" she asked, her lips pressed firmly together.

This was not going to be easy without sounding like some jerk. "We are mates."

"That much I know."

"My father is the king of all of Feyrion, which means at some point in the future, as the eldest son, I will be king."

"I see."

He inhaled. "Which means you will be queen."

Tory shook her head. "Me? I don't see a dragon shifter as a Fairy queen."

He let go of her hands. "That was why when you first arrived on Feyrion, close to death, my mother decided it would be best to slowly groom you for the position. It will take years though."

She held up her hands. "You're not making any sense. Years for what?"

"For your magical power to develop enough in order for you to rule."

Her eyes widened. "You really think I am going to turn into a Fairy when I mate with you? No offense, but I will not let anything jeopardize my dragon status."

He was mucking this up. "You won't. Trust me, you'll never turn into little points of light like my sisters."

"Then what?" Her patience appeared to be wearing thin.

"You'll have enough power to do what you did today—like hold up your hand and shove someone backward—whenever you want."

Tory bit down on her lip. "If what you say is true—that your mother plans to groom me to be queen—how can she do that if I live here?"

"She doesn't have to be here. She already inserted her magic inside you." He rushed on before she could object. "Think of it like a seed of magic if you will. She did that when I was giving you part of my life light."

Her mouth opened. Tory jumped up from the seat and nearly crashed into him. "What? I know most people would be grateful to be given all this power, but if this occurred months ago, why didn't you tell me then? Is there anything else you've lied about?"

Kenton stood. When he tried to take hold of her shoulders, she shrugged out of his grasp. "Tory, you weren't ready to learn you were possibly going to be the queen of a realm."

"Maybe not then, but a little hint would have helped. I've been going crazy thinking something is growing inside of me." Her voice had escalated.

"What do you mean?"

"I'm faster. It's almost as if I can teleport. Only I can't really."

It was happening. "It's natural."

"Natural? Is it natural for someone to implant something in my body without my permission? I can understand you giving me your life light. I mean, you were trying to save my life."

"I was."

"But to erase my memory and expect me to be okay with being set up as a future queen when I had no idea who you were is not acceptable."

When she put it that way, it might have been a mistake to do both rituals at the same time. "I'm sorry."

"You suck, you know that."

Tory stormed off. The front door slammed. Well, fuck.

Chapter Twenty

TORY SAW RED. When she was unconscious, it made sense that Kenton would do everything in his power to save her, but deciding she'd be queen without asking her? That was the last straw.

Needing to clear her head, Tory decided a long flight back to Edendale might help. She ran down the path toward the eternal flame in order to reach the path that would take her out of the woods. Before she reached it though, she was in her living room at home. Tory spun around. "What the hell?"

She had to be hallucinating. This couldn't be real. Tory touched the back of the sofa. It was solid. Had she just teleported? Given the time lapse, it was the only thing that made sense. But how? Was this yet another power his mother put in her? Kenton said it could take years to develop. Well, it had only been two months.

Wanting to test her abilities, Tory closed her eyes and pictured her bedroom. When she opened them again, she was still in the living room. So much for being able to teleport at will.

Now she was more confused than ever. What she needed was a stiff drink, but this time she wouldn't go to Wings. Kai might show up there. Besides, she might have more hidden powers inside of her that could harm innocent people.

She snapped her fingers. Wait. Angelique could help figure out what was going on, or would the Four Sisters be better able to help her? Since the root of the problem was with her not-so-truthful mate, the Four Sisters it was.

Not wanting to attempt the teleporting thing without instruction, she slowly walked out of her house, shifted, and flew to her destination. It was possible her heightened emotions had triggered her teleporting abilities.

It was still during business hours, so hopefully one of the four women would be able to help her. Inside, Poppy and Primrose were manning the store. Both sisters looked up and smiled. Poppy rushed over. "Tory, this is a surprise. I'm sorry we missed you the last time you stopped by."

Acacia must have mentioned her visit. "Can we talk?" Tory glanced over to the customer with Primrose. "It's kind of delicate."

"Of course. Come into the back and tell me what is troubling you."

Once out of sight and earshot of the others, Tory sat at the same table as before. "It's about my mate, Kenton Forrester."

Her eyes twinkled. "He's a fine man."

"Yes, but he's withheld information from me that is quite troubling." Tory told her about how he'd implanted his life light into her. During her discussion, Tory had the distinct impression that Poppy already knew all of that. "Yesterday, we spent the day in Feyrion where I met his mother, Queen Arianna." Tory waited for Poppy to react, but she did not. "Did you know about her?"

"About their mother being the queen?"

"Yes."

"I did."

When Poppy just sat there with a pretty smile, Tory continued. "After a wonderful sightseeing tour, we returned home only to be met by one of the Gromley demons."

Poppy's mouth opened. "That must have been scary, but I'm glad to see no harm came to you."

"Not to me." She explained about how the demon tried to poison Kenton. "When I held out my hands and yelled at him to stop, I must have created some kind of force field or something. It threw the demon backward."

"Very interesting. Did you ask Kenton about it?"

Interesting? That was all? "Yes, but he just said that my newfound powers had been his mother's doing, that she had put something inside me to help me become the next queen."

Poppy reached across the table and grabbed Tory's wrist, her eyes full of joy. "You're a Fey?"

"More like a Fairy. At least, I think. I honestly didn't stay around long enough to learn all of the details."

Poppy grinned. "I think it's wonderful—not the leaving part, but the Fairy part."

Was it? "Kenton said I'll always be a dragon, albeit one with a lot of power."

She leaned back. "I'm not sure I see the problem then."

Was she kidding? "The problem is that Kenton and his mother did this without asking my approval."

"Hmm."

Poppy's response wasn't helping. "What should I do?"

"Do you want to spend the rest of your life with Kenton?" Poppy asked.

The more time Tory spent with him, the more she wanted him. "I thought I did even though we haven't known each other for long. It's just that the lies don't seem to end."

"You are fated mates. Nothing can change that. Do you want my opinion?"

"Yes, it is why I came."

Poppy tapped her nails on the table. "Go back to Kenton and tell him exactly how you feel."

"He knows I'm mad."

"You need to figure out the source of your anger then. You have to decide if you are merely scared or if you feel he treated you unjustly."

Poppy might be right. Clearly defining her objections would be best. It was what any Guardian would do. "Fine. I'll take tonight to think, and then I'll approach him."

"Good."

"Oh, there is one other thing. One second I was in at the eternal flame and the next I was in my house. And I didn't fly there. I teleported."

"Really?"

"Yes, but I can't do it on command yet," Tory said.

Tory reached over and patted her hand. "Give it time. If you want me to work with you, I'd be happy to. You've met Ivy, right?"

"Yes, she's Jace's mate."

"She is. Ivy came from Earth to learn how to control her teleporting abilities, and I was able to help her."

Relief washed through her. "I might take you up on that offer."

Poppy pushed back her chair. "I hope you do."

While Tory wasn't sure how much meeting with Poppy helped, she did feel better.

KENTON PACED HIS living room. "I messed up, brother."

Bevon grabbed two beers and handed him one. "She's upset, that's all. You never warned her that her powers would arrive someday—and apparently without warning. That was your choice. In retrospect, it might not have been the right one."

"I know that now. You should have seen the force with which she shoved back that demon. It surprised even her. I think going to Feyrion triggered something."

"What are you going to do about it?" Bevon asked.

"I'm going to talk to her. She ran out of here in a huff. She was upset and probably confused."

Bevon walked into the living room, dropped down onto the sofa, and then propped up his feet. At least one of them was comfortable. "You have that bracelet thing. You can ask if you can see her."

"Seriously? She'll say no. It would be better just to show up. If I can just hold her, I think I can get her to forgive me."

Bevon held up his drink in a salute. "Good luck with that. I'm just glad I have not yet found my mate."

That thought almost made Kenton smile. "I don't envy the woman you end up with."

"Appreciate the vote of confidence."

Kenton smiled for the first time in a while.

He stood and then inhaled deeply. It was time to face his mate. Kenton hoped he could say the right things. With a mental nod, he arrived outside of her house. When Kenton placed a palm on her front door, he could sense her. Kenton knocked, and then he waited. And waited some more. Could she sense he was the one at her door and was refusing to answer? If that were true, her powers might be stronger than even he imagined.

Kenton knocked again. "Tory, it's me, Kenton."

Footsteps sounded inside, and the door opened. She still had on the same outfit from this morning. "Yes?" Her tone came out quite terse.

"Come on, love, don't be like that. I know you're mad, but give me a chance to explain."

"It seems as if you do that all too often."

The image of them making love on Feyrion played in his mind's eye. "I don't think I was explaining or apologizing when we were enjoying ourselves in the lake or on the bed of frenlen needles."

Her cheeks colored. "Fine, come in, but know that I am pretty freaked out."

"I would be too. Not telling you was wrong, but I'll use the excuse of trying to find and then fend off a demon."

Tory tilted her head. "Today maybe, but you had plenty of time while we were on Feyrion to let me know what was going to happen to me."

"Guilty as charged." Her pain was seeping into his soul. Sharing their life light made them connected. He couldn't imagine what it would be like when they mated. "We need to talk. Can we sit down?"

"Sure, but I haven't forgiven you for lying."

"I totally understand. I haven't forgiven myself for that either, but can we put that aside for now? I'm really worried that the demon might come here to harm you, and I can't let that happen."

"Why come after us now? Was it because my family didn't help his kind way back when?"

Kenton sat on the sofa and patted the cushion next to him. "That's possible, but I know for sure that he wants to harm me. The worst thing he can do to me is harm you."

She then sat down next to him. "If he comes near me again, I'll just push him away like I did before. I don't think that herb stuff will affect me."

Kenton loved her can-do attitude. "True, but what if there are more than one? Can you be sure you can duplicate that force field thing on command? Powers can be sporadic at first."

She crossed her arms over her chest. "Like my ability to teleport that I could only do one time?"

He stilled. "You teleported. For real?" Kenton failed to keep the excitement from his voice.

"I did one time, but when I tried again, I wasn't able to."

He tried to think if anything like that had happened to him. "When I was a toddler, I really struggled with telekinesis."

"Moving objects using your mind?"

"Yes. No matter how much I focused, one time I could move a rock two inches and the next it would go flying." He had to chuckle at one not so pleasant memory. "Once, the rock flew through the castle window. Needless to say, my father was pissed."

A small smile lifted her lips. "I can only imagine." She lowered her arms and faced him. "How did you learn to control it?"

"Practice. I can see that I should have warned you about your abilities. In all honesty, I didn't think they would be triggered when you went to Feyrion. I swear I was going to tell you about it as soon as we returned, but we were interrupted before I could."

"You should think about the consequences before you change a person's life, you know."

He smiled. "You are an amazing woman, love."

"Don't call me that." Tory looked away.

Kenton reached out and turned her chin toward him. "Why? You are the love of my life."

She finally locked her gaze with him. "I'm not feeling the love today."

He leaned back. "Fair enough."

She huffed. "Did you really struggle at first to learn how to control your talents? You were born a Fey."

"Are you kidding? That's like asking a young child if he had to learn to walk. I remember one time, Bevon and I were getting ready for bed. Back then, we shared a room."

"The castle wasn't big enough?"

He laughed. "My parents wanted us to bond."

"They succeeded."

"They did. Anyway, one time I wanted to get dressed for bed and swept my hands to take off my clothes. Instead, I took off Bevon's."

She barked out a laugh, but quickly sobered. "That could prove embarrassing."

"I agree." His gut told him not to do it, but he swept a hand and removed his clothes.

Her eyes widened, and then Tory looked away. "You are wickedly bad." He put his clothes back on and then took off hers. "Kenton Forrester, dress me immediately."

"Are you sure?" *Please say no.* Before she had the chance to answer, he took off his clothes again. "See? Now we are both naked, so you don't have to be embarrassed." Not that he thought she would be.

She crossed her one arm over her chest and kept the other arm on her lap. "You think you can come in here after lying to me and expect me to fall at your feet and make love to you just because you are naked?"

If her eyes hadn't turned purple and her scales hadn't been flashing bright yellow, he would have clothed them immediately. He reached out and slowly lowered her arms. He had no doubt that his eyes were pure gold. When her gaze dropped to his cock, followed by a deep inhale of breath, he'd say the answer was close to a yes.

"Why, yes I do, love."

Chapter Twenty-One

TORY WAS SO torn. She wanted to remain furious at Kenton. It would be easier for sure, but she could no more deny him than she could stop breathing. After his near-death experience, she realized that if he'd died, she would be lost forever. Considering he was naked—gloriously so—it was more or less a done deal. Why not take a slice of happiness now? She could always resume being mad at him later.

"You are confident," she said as she straddled him. The moment her body pressed against his hard cock, all clear thoughts escaped. It didn't matter. Enjoyment first, rational thinking later.

"I don't need confidence. I can read you like a book."

She groaned. "Where did you learn that terrible expression?"

His cheer seemed to evaporate. "At the coffee shop."

He was too much. "For someone so powerful, your interpersonal skills need some honing."

His cheer reappeared. "You are just the woman to help me. Once we mate, I will be able to sense your mood and act accordingly."

"Really? Will I be able to tell what you're thinking too?"

He ran his hands down her shoulders, his gaze on her breasts. "You won't need to read my mind. I'll make it obvious." Kenton pulled her forward just enough for his mouth to reach her right breast. He licked and suckled until every one of her nerves were on fire.

Wanting to let him know that she was in full lust mode, Tory pulled off the tie that held his long hair, tossed it aside, and then dragged her fingers along his scalp. Oh, how she loved the silky texture. Kenton was not only powerful, he was kind and sexy as hell. His communication skills were a bit lacking, but with some work on her part, she could help him develop that talent.

When he switched to the other breast, her teeth sharpened. Tory had no idea when she had decided to mate with him, but it was time. It wasn't because she was about to become some magic-wielding dragon who would someday rule Feyrion. It was because she wanted to spend the rest of her life with Kenton Forrester. From what he said, it could be forever.

He grabbed her waist and lifted her up. It was clear what he wanted her to do. Thankfully, she wanted the same thing. How he would mate with her, she didn't know, but he'd figure it out once she bit him. Needing to help him aim his cock, she grabbed hold and slid down onto him. His eyes flashed gold as his mouth opened.

"You feel so damned good." His voice almost sounded like a croak.

Tory leaned over and kissed him, his lips pliable yet demanding at the same time. As opposed to the last time they were together, she was the one who demanded entrance. This first contact sent her soaring. Even though Kenton might deserve it, Tory could never stay mad at him. He was her world and the other half of her heart and soul. She was never going to let him go.

Their tongues explored and tasted while she lifted up and then dropped back down on him, riding him hard. Just when she was on the brink of a climax, he held her hips still and drove up into her.

Their mating would change her life forever, which meant she should savor this moment. Too bad, she lacked the control. When she broke the kiss and dragged her lips to his neck, something strange occurred. His inner light grew brighter and brighter as a white haze blurred the edges of his body and encompassed her. Heat swamped her. As if she no longer had any control, she bit down on his neck. Love and light poured into her and heat infused every cell of her body. Tory could almost feel his power enter her.

When Kenton drove into her again, her orgasm exploded, briefly taking her back to the sweet-smelling forest on Feyrion. All troubles evaporated, and only the two of them existed.

As soon as Tory lifted her head, Kenton gave one last hard thrust and released his seed into her. Had this been in the past, she would have freaked that they hadn't used a condom. But today? It didn't matter. She licked his now-closing wound where she'd bitten him and sighed.

She sat back up, and the grin on his face made her smile. "You okay?" she asked, pretty sure she knew the answer.

"Never better." He lifted her off and set her on the sofa, but not before he magically created a cloth and placed it underneath her.

"I could get used to this," she said.

"That so?" He laughed. "It won't be long before you're just as powerful."

"If that's true, I'm sure I'll need a lot of practice."

He stroked her cheek. "I can help with that."

Tory leaned over and kissed him. "Thank you. Now how about we get dressed. If you stay naked for much longer, I'll have to have you again."

"And that is bad, why?"

She laughed. Life with Kenton would never be dull. "Just do it."

One second later, both were dressed. "As much as I would like for us to stay here in your very cozy home, we have something we have to take care of first."

"The demon?" she asked.

"The demon—or maybe the demons."

"Do you think cutting his throat would work?" she asked.

Kenton hesitated. "I would love to say yes, but I don't want to stake my life on it—or rather your life."

"You might be in danger if this demon could knock you out and then do something with that poisonous herb."

"That's probably true, but I am more or less an immortal."

"Except when Treniam is present."

"Unfortunately, yes."

She didn't want to think about the fact that he could die. "What about that magic ball that might destroy this demon. Why not use that?"

"My mother is working on it as we speak, assuming Tally agrees to help."

She'd heard a few comments about this elusive sister. "What is her story?"

"She likes it better on Feyrion."

Now wasn't the time to push. "You seem worried."

"I am a bit. Over the centuries this demon has learned to adapt to this magic ball that my sisters will make. What once worked to kill his kind might not kill them now."

This was so frustrating. "I guess if his kind were constantly being killed by these magic balls, the demon would have a need to adapt. But if no one has made one in a long time…"

He smiled. "There would be no need to change."

"Exactly," she said.

"What do you say we go back to the woods and speak with my sisters? They will need to take a little trip to Feyrion unless Tally comes here. To put my mind at ease, I'll put a cloaking spell on the cabin just in case some demon comes sniffing around. When you're there, you and the rest of us will be able to see it, but the demon won't see us."

A ton of thoughts bombarded her. "Can I become invisible too? I am able to cloak myself when I'm in my dragon form, so maybe now I can do that in my human form as well since we've mated." She was unable to hide her excitement.

Kenton laughed. "Maybe."

Without warning, he disappeared. Kenton was probably trying to demonstrate that he could cloak himself at will. However, she bet if she felt around she'd find him. Or was he like a ghost? There was only one way to find out. She leaned forward and waved her arms, hitting something solid.

Kenton appeared again and smiled. "Invisible but not gone.

Remember that."

"I will."

"I'd like to try teleporting to the forest," she said.

Kenton took her hands in his. "How about I give you some pointers when we have more time? If you do manage to teleport and mess up, you'd have to find a place to shift and then fly back to the forest."

He had a point. "Fine."

Kenton smiled. *"Want to pack a few things? I don't know how long we'll be gone?"* he telepathed.

While they had been able to communicate like this when she held onto her bracelet, they hadn't been able to do so without it. *"Okay."*

She smiled, slipped her hands out of his and stood. Tory pulled her phone from her pocket to let Greer know she wouldn't be coming into work for a few days.

"Are you letting Greer know?" Kenton asked.

"Yes. Can you read my mind now?"

He tapped his head and smiled. "Maybe. I'm a Fey after all."

Okay, that was a bit scary. Greer's cell went to voicemail, so she just left her a message. "We ran into the demon. Kenton scared him off, but I'm on my way to Feyrion to figure out a way to get rid of him permanently. I'll be out of communication range for a while. Don't worry. I'm in good hands."

Next, she called her mom, whose cell also went to voicemail. Wasn't anyone picking up? Maybe it was for the best. It would have taken some time to convince her mom that she would be safe. She left the same message as she had for Greer.

Kenton placed a hand on her shoulder and smiled. "I'm sure both will appreciate the heads up."

Once Tory packed, they teleported to the forest. This time they landed inside the cabin. She faced him. "Just to be clear. Can anyone just walk in here?"

"Not without being invited. That means this is a no-demon

zone."

Relief rushed through her. "Good to know."

Kenton slipped her bag from her fingers. "I'll put this in the bedroom." He returned quickly. "Ready to go to Feyrion?" he asked.

"What about Bevon?"

"I just telepathed him and explained our plan. He and the two guards will make sure no demons get through the portals. I also asked Meena and Fay to join us at our Feyrion home."

Tory wrapped her arms around his neck. "I have to say that this telepathing thing is certainly more efficient than phones."

"Eventually, you'll be able to communicate with anyone in the realm."

She lowered her arms. "Anyone? Not just your family."

"Anyone, but no one would dare interrupt your mind unless something critical had occurred." He wrapped an arm around her. "Let's focus on the here and now, shall we?"

"What about my suitcase? Shouldn't I take it with us?"

Kenton stepped back, swept a hand up and down her body. Air brushed her skin. When she looked down, she was stunned. "I was wearing black jeans and a pink top. Now I have on blue jeans and a green top. How did you do that?"

"It's magic, love."

Tory wasn't sure she'd ever be able to get used to that. In reality, Tory shouldn't be too surprised. He was able to pluck a condom out of thin air. "So it appears."

As much as she wanted to ask why she bothered to pack in the first place, she figured he had his reasons.

Kenton held out his hand. "The portal is out back."

"When we arrived the last time, it was in front."

"We often move it. Ever since the demon made his appearance, I've been switching it up. Come on."

She wasn't about to argue. He swept a hand to create a portal, saying a few words—words that she'd have to learn. After stepping through it, they were in Feyrion. The light was brighter and the colors richer, making her smile once more.

Kenton looked down at her. "Let's say hi to my folks—assuming dad is here—and then get together with my sisters. It's time you met Tally."

Chapter Twenty-Two

KENTON TELEPATHED TO his family to join Tory and him in the palace's front room. By the time the two of them arrived, all five of his family were there. He smiled, but the tension rippling through Tory unnerved him a bit.

"They will love you. Relax," he telepathed.

She looked up at him and smiled. That seemed to do the trick. His mother rushed up to them and hugged Tory and then him. "You're back so soon."

"We need the magic ball," Kenton said.

His mother smiled. "Of course."

Tally stepped up next and introduced herself. His father was next, but as soon as he greeted Tory, he gave some reason why he had to rush off.

Meena smiled. "I know, brother, that you don't want to be gone from the portal for too long, so we should get started in making that magic ball."

Good old Meena. She was the peacekeeper of the family. "I appreciate that." He nodded to his mother. "If you'll excuse us. Tory and I have some training to do while you and my sisters create your magic."

He teleported to the glen that was surrounded by the forested area where they'd had their splendid interlude.

Tory laughed. "I think we need to have some kind of warning signal. It's a bit disconcerting to be standing in one spot and then be whisked off to another a second later. And be forewarned. As soon as I learn to teleport, I'm going to do that to you." Tory faced him, wrapped her arms around his waist, and pulled him close. "Okay?"

He laughed, loving his mate more each day. "I'll be ready, but I did kind of warn you when I told my mother we were about to train."

She smiled. "Fine, but we should set up a signal."

"I get it. You want to be told. I'll do that for the next time."

"Thank you. What are we training for first? Teleporting?"

His mate was always so refreshing. "I thought we'd try cloaking first, which was why I took us to the glen. It's totally open and you can shift into your dragon form first if need be."

"Why would I want to do that?"

"I've never trained anyone to do this, but I think cloaking yourself while in your dragon form first and then shifting into your human form would be easiest."

Her eyes widened in understanding. "That would be incredibly useful if I can stay invisible in my human form even after I shift."

No doubt, Tory was picturing herself as a Guardian. "Give it a try."

She stepped into the middle of the field, and when she shifted, Kenton couldn't help but stare. She was even more beautiful than the first time he had seen her flying overhead. Her intense yellow scales were glorious in contrast to her darker ones. Before he finished admiring her, she had disappeared.

"I'm in my cloaked dragon form," she telepathed.

"I can see that—or rather I can't see that. Now try shifting into a human."

"Wish me luck."

She didn't need luck. Tory had magic on her side. When nothing happened, he figured something had malfunctioned returning to her human form. *"Can a cloaked dragon shift back into a human?"* he asked.

Instead of answering, hands grabbed his waist and breasts pressed against his back. Kenton spun around in her grasp but saw no one.

"Yes, I can." Tory then appeared, dropped her head back and

laughed. "That was so cool."

Kenton lifted her up and spun her around. "It was. Now go from visual human to invisible human without the intermediate step."

She bit down on her lip. "Do I just picture being cloaked?"

He had to think about that. "I guess. I just command my body to do it."

"No password or chant?"

"Nothing, my love. Becoming invisible for a Fey is built into our brain."

She inhaled. "I'll try."

One minute she was in front of him, and the next she wasn't. Technically, she was still in front of him, but he couldn't see her. Tory then reappeared. Kenton couldn't help but lean over and kiss her. "You did it!"

"I did."

"I am proud of you. We'll turn you into a Fey after all." He stroked her cheek. "Do you think I will inherit any of your dragon capabilities?"

"I don't know. Magnolia—one of the Four Sisters of Fate—was the only one of the four to inherit her mate's shifter abilities." She cupped his face. "But let's give it a try."

While Kenton no longer relished becoming king, because he now had Tory, if he could become a dragon, his status would be elevated. "How do I do it?"

"Close your eyes and picture a dragon—me, maybe."

That was easy enough. He shut them tight. "Now what?"

"I too have never taught anyone to shift, but maybe start running and flap your wings—I mean arms that will hopefully turn into wings."

"Seriously? I'll look ridiculous."

Tory smiled and shook her head. "No one is here but me. How about I turn around and close my eyes?"

Kenton never worried about looking like an idiot before, but this was his mate. "That might work."

She faced the other direction, and he had to assume she'd closed her eyes. Kenton closed his for a moment to center himself. When he was ready, he opened them and ran, raising and lowering his arms. He imagined soaring high in the air with the wind beneath him. Even after ten seconds at a full out sprint, nothing happened, and his tight control started to crack. He teleported back to Tory. "You can open your eyes."

"Did it work?"

"What do you think?"

She pressed her cheek against his chest, and that one little action soothed the beast that clearly didn't want to come out.

Tory leaned back. "We'll start with something smaller. Try this."

She stepped back and held out her arms. A second later, her elbow down to her fingertips turned into a giant claw, and she shot fire out of the end.

"Wow," he exclaimed.

Her arms and hands transformed back to human. "If I can send a man hurtling fifty feet, you can shoot fire. This should be easy for you."

He inhaled. Not wanting to disappoint her, Kenton extended his hands, and concentrated on what her arms looked like. Seconds later, fire shot out of his fingertips—make that his still very Fey fingertips—and his pulse soared. "I can't believe it."

When he lowered his arms, he forgot about turning off the fire, and it was only when the grass sent up a puff of smoke that he mentally turned it off. Kenton grinned but Tory didn't look happy.

She touched his forearm. "Your arms didn't change into scales." She checked his palms and then ran a finger across it. "They're not even hot."

That was true. "I think my body adapted. I guess I'll have to be content to be a hybrid. That's okay. I have enough power without being able to fly."

She ran a hand down his chest. "Let's not give up. It might just take time."

Kenton stroked her face. "I mean it. It's okay, love. I'll let you be the one in the family to fly."

"It would have been fun if we both could have flown together, but when I learn to teleport, we can do that instead."

He loved her attitude. Correction—he loved everything about her. "That's true, but I think we've had enough magic for today. It's not like we can't return anytime we want. We need to deal with the demons, and I don't want Bevon to fight that battle alone."

"I know."

"We're finished with the magic ball," Fay telepathed. *"Meena and I are heading back to Tarradon. No telling if Bevon might need it first."*

Tory's eyes widened and then a grin spread across her face. She must have heard them. *"We'll be back soon, too. Thank you."*

Once he mentally shut off that connection, he faced Tory. "You heard?"

"I did. I guess we are all linked. It's strange and almost creepy at the same time. Can they read my thoughts?"

"Not really. Even if they could, they wouldn't. It's not who the Fairies are."

"Good to know," she said.

"We should head back to Tarradon."

"I thought we were going to stay here a few days," she said. While it didn't come as a whine, he could sense her disappointment. Part of him was thrilled she enjoyed Feyrion so much. Not giving Tory what she wanted, hurt him.

"Like I said, I don't want to leave Bevon to defend the portal in case the demons return."

"Why did we come here then? Your sisters and mother could have made the magic ball without you."

She was smart. "True, but we came because our magic is stronger on Feyrion. I thought it would be easier for you to learn to cloak yourself and easier for me to shift if we were here." He smiled. "One out of two isn't bad."

Tory rubbed his arm. "You can create fire. That's a start."

"You're right. Ready to go back?"

"I am."

With a hand on her, he teleported them to the portal where two guards were standing watch. They opened the portal, allowing them to step into Tarradon. Always in need of changing the exit location, they landed closer to the eternal flame than before.

"This is different," Tory said as she looked around.

"Makes it harder for the unwelcomed ones to find us. Would you prefer walking or teleporting?" he asked.

She inhaled deeply. "I'd love to hold your hand and walk. While Feyrion is amazing, this forest is enchanted in a different way."

He laughed. "I think you are right."

Instead of going to his house, he stopped at his sisters' place first. He needed that magic ball. Out of politeness, he knocked first. Meena answered and her brows rose. "Such formality. Do come in."

"May I see our object of destruction?" he asked, putting some cheer in his voice.

Meena disappeared and then reappeared carrying what could best be described as a very small sun about a foot in diameter. He ran his hand over the surface. "It's not even hot."

"No, but with the right speed and aim, it will kill a demon. At least Mom said it would."

"May I?" Tory asked.

"By all means."

Very carefully she reached out and was able to stick her hand right through the light. "How can that hurt anyone if it has no substance?"

He loved her naiveté. "That's where the magic comes in. I'll say a few words before I toss it. That is what will give it it's deadly power."

"Could it kill a dragon?" she asked.

Kenton looked over at his sisters. When they didn't answer, he lifted a shoulder. "Never tried it on one."

"So now what?" she asked.

"It won't do me any good if it's in here. I'll carry it outside, place it in a convenient spot, and then cloak it. When the time comes, I will use it to destroy the demon."

"How can you be so sure you'll have the chance?" she asked. "The last time he teleported close enough to touch you."

Kenton stroked her face. "Then I will have to be sure to throw it at him before he has the chance to do that. Come on."

Handling the magic ball with care, Kenton carried it outside. "I need to let Bevon know where it is should he be the one to need it."

She looked around. "Where is your brother, anyway?"

"Good question. I'll ask him." Kenton focused on Bevon. *"What are you up to?"* he telepathed. *"Tory and I just returned from Feyrion. I have the magic ball and am ready to take down Kai."*

"Great. I'm with a couple of our guys looking for the Treniam."

"Good. We need to have that stuff eradicated."

"I couldn't agree more."

Kenton turned back to Tory, but she'd disappeared. *"Trying to practice disappearing on me?"*

"Yes," she telepathed back. *"Can't see me, can you?"*

"Nope." He could if he wanted to though, but he wanted her to think she was invincible. In time, she'd have that same talent of detecting another cloaked family member as they all did.

With a smile, Kenton placed the ball along the path and cloaked it. He was just about to suggest he teach her about the portals when a man appeared. The fact Kenton's body was vibrating implied this was another demon. Well, fuck.

Chapter Twenty-Three

TORY FROZE. FROM the way Kenton's body had stiffened, this newcomer was not someone friendly, and she hoped like hell it wasn't a demon. It wasn't Kai, which for some reason scared her even more. If he was a demon, how many of them were there on Tarradon?

Her body started to vibrate, causing one of her hands to appear and then disappear. Crap. The last thing she needed was for her cloaking abilities to up and leave. Being on Tarradon might be affecting her.

As quietly as she could, Tory hid behind a tree. Since she was now hidden, she mentally allowed the cloak to release its hold. Immediately, energy trickled back into her body. She shouldn't be surprised to learn it took work to hold the cloaking. It was the same as when she was in her dragon form.

"What do you want?" Kenton asked the stranger.

"Just came to chat. We have a friend in common. Malakai Gromley."

Tory almost let out a gasp. Kenton glanced over to the spot where he'd cloaked the magic ball, and Tory prayed he'd get it in time before this other monster attacked. What Kenton needed was a distraction. About the only thing she'd ever done was hold out her hands and somehow force some magical power out of her fingertips that could hurl a person backward. She now believed her ability to do this must have been an extension of her shooting fire out of her arms, since the same movement was involved.

"Kenton, I can distract him," she said.

"That would be great. Anytime, love."

Tory cloaked herself once more and as quietly as possible moved toward the man's back. If she sent him hurtling away from her though, he might fly into Kenton, so Tory moved to the side. Once she was situated, she held out her arms and mentally told this demon to stop.

Nothing happened.

Damn it.

The last time she'd succeeded, she'd been terribly angry and afraid. The man pulled some of those terribly poisonous weeds out of his pocket and waved the sprig at Kenton. Fear, panic, anger, and a host of other emotions all slammed into her at once. Her body heated. Her heart raced. Full of anguish, she grit her teeth and pictured the man hurtling through the air. She held out her hands once more. As if her wish was her command, the man tumbled to the side and doing two somersaults before landing on his hands and knees. While she hadn't done much damage, it gave Kenton enough time to retrieve the ball. He lifted it over his head and threw it at the downed man. The demon did nothing to stop it. It was as if the light either mesmerized or paralyzed him.

One minute the demon's eyes were wide open, and the next the light from the ball faded, leaving a shell of a demon behind.

"What the hell?" said a voice from off to the side.

She spun around. Oh, no. It was Kai! Fearing her ability to remain cloaked wouldn't hold, she searched for the nearest tree to hide behind. All she found was a bush. *"Distract him while I hide,"* she telepathed.

"Go."

Tory moved softly but quickly. Her heart was still in her throat when she reached the tree. Not wanting to use too much energy, she materialized. Thankfully, Kai's back was to her or he might have caught a glimpse of her. She could only hope he couldn't sense her, especially since she was now mated to a Fey.

"What do you want this time, Kai?" Kenton asked, acting bored, though she could sense he was anything but.

"I wasn't prepared the last time." From out of nowhere, he pulled a sword from his side. "I've come to make your demise final."

No, no, no. Kenton didn't stand a chance, or did he? Could a Fey die if Kai cut off his head? That thought sent chills down her body.

Think. There had to be something she could do. Before Tory came up with a plan though, Kenton lifted his arm and produced a sword of his own. Her pulse skyrocketed. That was amazing. Kenton charged. There went her plan to use force to send him on his way. She might have hurled Kenton instead.

She watched in awe as the two men dueled. It was an ancient art, but both men looked as if they practiced often. Whether Kenton became distracted or Kai got lucky she couldn't decide, but somehow the demon's blade sliced Kenton's arm. He swore and then stumbled backward. There wasn't much blood, but his pain bombarded her, like Kaleena's pain had nearly toppled her when she was giving birth.

Kenton lifted his sword, seemingly having his bearings. He attacked and cut Kai too. To her dismay, Kai seemed unfazed. That was so not good. Was it true that the only way to kill a demon was by using the magic ball of light or by cutting off its head? The ball no longer existed. That meant Kenton had to cut off this ass' head.

She wanted to shout encouragement, but she didn't want to give away her position. Kai struck again. This time the blade pierced Kenton's torso. Acid burned in her stomach at the inflicted injury. Tory was a Guardian, damn it. She should be able to help. While the trees were too low to shift, she could shoot fire at the bastard. The problem with that was she might burn Kenton in the process. She also wondered if fire would even harm Kai?

If only she had a sword, she'd cut off the jerk's head. As if she'd willed it, a sword appeared in her hand. She was so surprised, she almost dropped it.

Only then did a viable plan form. She would cloak herself, sneak up behind Kai, and swing the sword as hard as she could. Killing another dragon in battle had never been too hard, but to cut off a person's head would take all of her willpower.

Kai approached Kenton, swinging the blade over his head. Determination drove her. She was not going to let this…this freak of nature kill the man she loved.

Tory cloaked herself, and thankfully the sword disappeared from view too. Just as she stepped around the tree, someone else appeared. Only this time, the man had a red glowing head. He too was holding a sword.

Her dragon roared. When this newcomer demon rubbed the plant Treniam along the blade's edge, Tory just reacted. She didn't even care if she lost her cloaking. Nothing was going to stop her from killing this new demon.

The red-headed monster dropped the sprig of poison he'd just used and then lifted his sword. *Oh, no you don't.* With every ounce of her being, she went on the offensive. Sword held high over her head, she ran as fast as she could, her vision tunneling. To her shock, she teleported right behind him. Not allowing herself to even think, she took one hard swing, and the blade connected with the man's neck. Her sword must have been imbued with magic, because it went right through the skin and bones without any resistance.

The shock of seeing his head fly sickened her, which caused her to lose concentration. Tory's body appeared, and only then did she notice the crimson covered sword.

Kai stopped his attack. Kenton was already on his knees. From the way he was wincing, Kai's blade must have been covered in Treniam too.

Kai smiled. "Well, well. We meet again. I underestimated you."

Tory tightened her grip on the sword, ready to take his head also. Before she even was able to respond though, the light in Kai's face dimmed, and he disappeared.

"Tory," said a voice behind her.

She spun around. When she realized it was Bevon, she almost threw her arms around his neck, but Kenton needed her more.

"Kenton's hurt."

"I know." He closed his eyes for a moment. A few seconds later, Meena and Fay appeared by Kenton's side.

Crap. She should have telepathed them, but she'd totally forgotten about her new abilities. Tory ran to Kenton and knelt in front of him. His smile came out weak, and then he passed out.

"Do something." She'd practically yelled at his sisters.

Bevon, who was with two strangers, rushed over to his brother and picked him up. All of them then disappeared.

She hoped they were either in Kenton and Bevon's cabin or with Meena and Fay. After a quick search, Tory finally found them in Fay and Meena's cabin.

Since they were in the middle of some kind of spell, she merely watched as they once more tried to save her mate.

"How is he?" she telepathed to Bevon, not having any idea if she could communicate with him at will.

"It doesn't look good. The Treniam is taking its toll." From the way his hands were fisted, he wasn't hopeful.

"Kenton said your mother was all powerful. Can't she help?"

"She can under most circumstances. Before we call her, let's give my sisters a chance to do their magic."

This was terrible. "What if Kai returns?"

Bevon finally dragged his focus away from Kenton and motioned they go outside. Because he had placed a hand on her shoulder, they were on the porch in a flash. "Tell me what happened, so I can come up with a plan." Bevon said.

She explained the best she could. "Kai was good with a sword. When that other demon arrived, I cloaked myself and charged, sword swinging."

His mouth opened. "You cut off his head?"

He didn't have to act so surprised. She was a Guardian. "Yes."

"Where did you get the sword?"

"Does it matter?"

"I guess not. Then what?"

"Right before I attacked, I saw that beast rub Treniam on his sword. I figured that was why Kenton was struggling so much."

"Damn."

"Where have you been?" she asked, trying to keep the bitterness from her voice but failing. If Bevon had been there, they could have fought Kai and the other demon together.

One eyebrow rose. "Doing what Kenton wanted me to do. We located the Treniam crop and destroyed it. I knew the demon was here, but Kenton told me he had everything under control."

"Don't listen to him the next time." Kenton was too stubborn for his own good.

A very slight smile stole across Bevon's face. He then suddenly sobered. "Meena and Fay want us inside."

A second later, they were leaning over a very pale Kenton. Fay looked up. "We need to take him to Feyrion. We think the second dosage has overpowered his body. We've done all we can."

Tory refused to ask if he would die. She couldn't handle it if he did. "What can I do?" she asked.

"Be by my brother's side. He will be able to sense you."

"Of course."

Bevon once more lifted Kenton and then disappeared.

"Can you teleport?" Meena asked.

"Not reliably."

Meena reached out and clasped her hand. They were behind Bevon and Kenton in a flash. One of them must have created the portal because it appeared out of nowhere. Two steps later, they were in Feyrion, and pulses of hope shot through her. Their mother was very powerful. She had to be able to save her own son.

Tory ran up to Kenton and placed her hand on his forehead. One step later, they were inside the palace entranceway. His mother appeared before them. This teleporting stuff still unnerved her, but it was a miracle when time was of the essence.

"Let's go into the living room," their mother said. "I can treat him there."

Once there, Tory couldn't tell what Queen Arianna was doing other than she was holding her hands out over her son and mumbling something that was probably in the Feyrionian language.

"Please Kenton, wake up," Tory telepathed in the hopes she could reach him. Unfortunately, he didn't respond.

Their mother lowered her arms. "Girls, do you want to help?"

"We've tried, mother," Meena said. "I think it is more than just the poison running through his bloodstream."

"Is it possible the demon I killed implanted his essence into him?" Tory asked.

Bevon placed a hand on her shoulder. "If you came at him from behind and cut off his head, he wouldn't have had the time to do that."

"What about Kai then? Could he have left a trace of himself?" she asked.

Bevon glanced over at his brother. "It's possible. I suppose during the fight he could have transferred some of his being into Kenton. He might have decided to do whatever it took to make sure Kenton died."

"Tory might be right," his mother said. "While I can heal many people, this...this poison inside my son is spreading too fast."

Her mind shot back to when her brother Declan had encountered the same thing with a friend of Chelsea's back on Earth. "Would it be possible to bring my brother here? He's a healer, and he's dealt with demons before. I know he struggled to help my dad, but when he had help from a witch on Earth, they were able to exorcise one."

"A witch?" the Queen Arianna asked.

"Yes. She was the Four Sisters' grandmother." Tory lifted a hand. "You wouldn't know them, I realize, but they are—"

The queen moved closer. "Are you speaking about Ophelia?"

"Yes." Tory couldn't believe that she knew of this woman who lived in a different realm.

The queen smiled briefly. "Many know of her. So, you're saying that your brother, together with Ophelia, were able to eradicate a demon's soul inside of a person?"

"Yes."

"Then by all means let's ask him to come. I believe I can be the substitute for Ophelia. I sensed I was missing something, some power, some magic, and maybe your brother is just what I need, especially now that my son has some dragon in him." She looked up at Bevon. "Can you bring him to me?"

"It will be faster if Tory comes with me."

"Of course. I'll do anything," Tory said.

Bevon placed a hand on her shoulder. "Tell me where we might find this brother of yours."

Chapter Twenty-Four

TORY AND BEVON teleported to the SinCas building where they found Declan busy in his office. Thankfully, it didn't take much to convince him to help.

"You don't want Greer to come along?" he asked.

Tory had thought about it. "I think your healing abilities are better suited to rid a person's body of a demon."

"I couldn't help Dad. How can I help Kenton?"

"You had Ophelia before. Kenton's mom is just as powerful."

Declan set down his cup on his desk. "Let's go. Do I need to take anything with me?"

Bevon shook his head. "You'll be back here in no time. Ready?"

"We're really teleporting together?" her brother asked.

Tory hoped that wasn't an issue. "Yes. I know it's a bit disconcerting the first time you do it, but don't be afraid." That would get him to agree.

"I'm not afraid." Tory thought he let out a chuckle.

"We'll have to return to my cabin and then take the portal to our world," Bevon said.

He placed a hand on each of their shoulders, and instantly, they were standing in front of the cabin door that led to the portal.

Declan looked over at him. "You're right. It was a bit unsettling but exhilarating at the same time."

She smiled. "Wait until we get to the palace."

"The palace?"

He'd find out soon enough. Bevon had a glint in his eye right before he created the portal. Together, they stepped through. Most likely because the view of the countryside was so spectacular that he let them stand there for a moment. "Whoa." Her brother looked around.

"Enough sightseeing. Times a wasting," Bevon announced before he teleported them to the palace living room.

Poor Declan. All of this must be overwhelming.

"This is Queen Arianna of Feyrion," Tory said. "She is Kenton's mom."

He stepped over to her. "What do you need me to do?"

She loved her brother for getting straight to the point.

The queen explained about the poison and the possible demon interaction. "I'm not really sure what is going on, but even I couldn't heal my son. I need more power—or rather a different kind of power. Why don't you tell me what you need me to do? You've done this before."

Her admiration for Kenton's mother just shot through the roof. All she wanted to do was cure her son. Most of what Declan told Kenton's mom was said in a hushed voice. As much as Tory wanted to hold Kenton's hand, she didn't want to interfere with their process.

For the next twenty minutes, the two of them did chant after chant. Finally, the queen turned to her. "We've done all that we can."

Tory's heart nearly shattered. "What are you saying?" Kenton wasn't going to die. He couldn't.

"Stay with him. Talk to him. He'll be able to sense you. If my son is as strong as I believe him to be, he'll survive."

Tory was willing to do anything. "Of course."

Just as Bevon was pulling over a chair for her to sit next to Kenton, King Leighton appeared and stepped over to Kenton. "Son? Can you hear me?" He looked up at his wife. "Why didn't you tell me?"

The queen took hold of his elbow. When the king nodded, Tory figured they were telepathing and able to block out what they said to others. The king walked over to Tory and held out his hand. "Thank you for being with Kenton. I'm sorry I had to rush out when we met the last time. There has been some serious unrest in another part of the realm. I would have been here earlier if I had known."

She wasn't sure how to respond. "I understand."

"Leighton, darling, would you come with me?" the queen asked her mate.

"Coming, my love." He turned back to Tory. "I hope after Kenton wakes that we'll have some time to get to know each other."

"I'd like that," she said.

Bevon placed a hand on her shoulder. "I'll escort Declan back to Tarradon. Sit with Kenton. When you tire, I'll take over."

He was a sweet man. "Thank you."

Before Declan left, she hugged him. "I appreciate you coming."

"I'm still in a bit of shock. I think we helped. Please let me know when he wakes up."

She reached up and kissed his cheek. "I will."

And then he was gone. Tory rushed back over to Kenton, ready for the long wait.

KENTON OPENED HIS eyes and stilled. Why was he in the palace living room, and why was Tory sitting next to him with her eyes closed and her head down? He ran a hand over his stomach, but no injury appeared to be there. He had been in a fight with Kai, right? Being this confused upset him.

"Tory?" He asked it out loud, because he didn't want to jar her too quickly by telepathing.

She jerked awake. The smile that bloomed radiated with love. "Kenton! You're alive."

It took him a moment to recall why she would think that. "Of course, I am."

She placed a hand on his. "What do you remember about the demon fight?"

As if she'd opened the flood gates to his memory, everything came rushing back. The pain, the weakness, and then the darkness. "Kai did this."

"Yes."

"I guess I'm here because neither Meena nor Fay could heal me back on Tarradon."

"It took your mother and my brother Declan to rid your body of not only the poison, but of the demon presence as well."

"Declan helped? How? He couldn't help your father."

"I know, but that's because he needed to work with your mother. Only by combining their talents were they able to heal you."

"Well, I'll be." He sat up. While he was a bit weak, Kenton wasn't experiencing much residual effect from the battle. "They did a good job."

She grinned. "You're really going to be okay?"

He eased his legs off the sofa and slowly stood. After trying to ignore the head rush, he gathered Tory in his arms. "I am now."

Her hold tightened, and when she leaned her head back, those lips called to him. Kenton wanted nothing more than to kiss her.

"Ahem." Drat. It was his mother.

He let go of his mate, spun around, and smiled. His mother opened her arms and rushed toward him. *"How are you feeling? Really?"* she telepathed, though he didn't know why she didn't speak out loud.

"I'm good."

She stepped back and scanned him from head to toe. "You don't feel any evil swirling inside you?"

"No, but I am working hard to control my anger. I want those bastards gone from both Feyrion and Tarradon. They have caused enough damage."

"You and me both. If I recall, there is a spell that sent them packing hundreds of years ago. I need to locate it, so we can send them back to Cargonia for another four hundred years."

"I'd prefer for eternity, but I'll take a few hundred."

His mother nodded. "Let me search the library. I'll be back shortly."

As soon as she disappeared, he turned back to Tory. His beautiful mate had dark circles under her eyes. "How long was I out?"

"Almost a day."

He ground his teeth. "They will pay for this."

Tory placed a hand on his arm. "Bevon told me that he and some others destroyed the crop of Treniam on Tarradon."

"That's a relief. I wish I knew how many demons were on Tarradon."

"We know of at least three, but only one is alive. That would be Kai," she said.

"Yes. Kai the coward." Out of the corner of his eye, he'd seen the head of one roll. "Were you responsible for the demise of one of them?"

She grinned. "Why, yes I was." She told him how a sword had miraculously appeared in her hand, and that it wasn't an ordinary sword. "When I cut off his head, it was like I was slicing through butter. I figured it was imbued with magic."

"It was, and you, Tory Sinclair, are a special woman. I can understand why Fate paired us together."

His mother appeared waving a book in her hand. "Good news. I found the spell, but it will take four women to do it. I would ask my daughters to assemble here, but it needs to be done in each realm."

"Do you think Tory is ready?" he asked.

Tory slapped a hand on her chest. "Me? I can't do a spell."

His mom smiled. "Leave that to me. I'm an excellent teacher."

TO SAY TORY was nervous was an understatement. What if she messed up? After all, Meena, Fay, and Tally were really Fairies, and she'd only been taught the spell a few hours ago. "Are you guys sure this will work?" she asked.

Meena placed a hand on Tory's arm. "No, but we're going to do our best."

Then they were in one of Kenton's sisters' living room. Fay had told Kenton that he had to wait in his cabin, saying he'd only be a distraction. That worked for Tory.

"Okay," Tally said. "The six candles have been lit, and the herbs from various flowers are connecting those candles."

"I've never seen anyone use candles before," Tory said.

"This is a special spell," Tally said.

Tory guessed Tally might be the most powerful one since she preferred to stay on Feyrion. Tally had only agreed to return to Tarradon this time to help banish the Gromley demons back to Cargonia after learning what they had done to Kenton.

Meena held out both hands, and the other two followed. Tory did the same. Being part of something so powerful thrilled and scared her at the same time. Tory's pulse was racing, but her stomach was remarkably calm. Maybe this was where she was meant to be.

All three sisters huddled close to her so they could read from this ancient book. With a nod, the chanting began. There were so many questions Tory wanted to ask about what she was reciting, but she understood that it would be best if she waited until after the ceremony.

The women kept repeating the same three phrases over and over again. While it had apparently been translated into Tarradonian many years ago, it still made little sense. But Tory was a team player, and she'd keep repeating the phrases until the sisters told her to stop.

The candles flickered, and then something miraculous happened. The herbs that connected the candles began to move. Tory held her breath and watched as the lines of herbs reached the center. They then disappeared. What the hell?

Then the candles extinguished, seemingly all on their own. Tory was in awe and freaked out at the same time.

Meena smiled. "It is done. The demons are back where they belong."

While Tory wasn't totally convinced, she wasn't about to argue with them. "Thank you so much." She turned to Tally. "And thank you for coming here."

Tally nodded. "You all needed me."

The silence that followed was a bit awkward. "I guess, I'll get back to Kenton," Tory said.

Meena stepped up next to her. "You do know that without you and your brother, we might have lost him."

Tory hadn't thought about it in those terms before. "I'm glad the both of us could help."

"We three will return to Feyrion, and with our mother, we'll do this spell again just in case there are any Gromley demons there," Meena said.

"That's great."

Wanting to see her love, Tory concentrated on teleporting to Kenton's cabin. She did succeed in changing locations, but instead of his cabin, she ended up at the eternal flame. Well shit.

Either she could walk the twenty minutes back to the cabin, take another crack at it, or ask Kenton to come get her. Since she wanted to see him, she telepathed her request. In seconds, he was next to her.

"Hi," he said as he leaned down and kissed her. "How did it go?"

"Thank you for not asking why I'm at the eternal flame."

Kenton placed a hand on his chest. "I figured you wanted to check it out again."

Tory laughed. "You know very well that isn't the case. I tried teleporting all of what, thirty feet? And instead I ended up here. I'm hopeless."

Kenton gathered her in his arms. "You are anything but hopeless. First, tell me about the spell, and then we can see about honing a few of your other skills."

Only because he winked did she assume he meant her skills in the bedroom. "Be serious."

Kenton laughed. "I am. I can feel your tension and wanted to help relax you." He snapped his fingers. "I have the perfect solution."

"What's that? Are you going to give me a backrub?"

"Hmm. That has a lot of potential, but you'd have to be naked, and once that happened, I wouldn't last but a minute before my lust consumed me."

"You're right. What's the plan?"

"Tell me about the spell."

Tory outlined how the four of them said the spell in unison, and soon the herbs began to move. "It was almost as if some other entity was in the room with us." She stilled. "Did one of the sisters use telekinesis to move the leaves in order to convince me the demons were gone?"

Kenton cupped her face. "No. They want the demons gone just as much as you and I do. If the leaves moved, then it was the spell that did it."

Tory blew out a breath. "What can we do to be sure Kai and any of his other friends are gone?"

"I asked Bevon to check it out. I believe he even plans to enlist the help of Declan."

That made her happy. "I really appreciate you asking my family. I think it is really important that we are united."

"Precisely. Now that the threat is at least temporarily, if not permanently, gone, I know of a perfect spot to go."

"Where is that?"

"You'll just have to trust me, but first I want to grab a few towels."

What was he up to? Whatever it was, she was sure it would be incredible because Kenton Forrester was the most amazing man alive.

Chapter Twenty-Five

KENTON HAD SPOTTED the hot springs a few months ago after he'd done some scouting in Thedia Province. While the air was chillier than he preferred, it made it even nicer to be in the steaming water.

"Is this helping to relax you?" he asked. Tory was leaning her head back against the rock-faced pool, and her legs were floating in the water.

Tory moaned. "This is so what I needed." She reached under the water and squeezed his leg. "Thank you."

"After what you've been through, it was the least I could do."

"Brother, we are in the clear," Bevon telepathed.

"You checked everywhere?"

"Declan and I didn't have to. Mother temporarily gifted us with a spell to mentally search all of Tarradon. I can assure you the demons are all gone."

"That is great news," Kenton responded. *I'm assuming, she will do the same on Feyrion?"*

"Yes, she will. Mom is very excited about the new spell book—or rather ancient spell book—that she found."

He could only imagine what trouble she might get into. For the most part, his mom acted like the queen she was, but at times, she liked to cut loose. *"I'll tell Tory the good news."*

Kenton faced her and smiled. He told her about his mom's gift to Bevon. "My brother and yours found no evidence of any demons."

She swung around and hugged him. "That is fantastic. That

means we can get on with our lives."

"I'd like nothing more." He leaned over and kissed her.

She pressed on his chest. "We can't get started. This is a public hot spring."

Kenton smiled. "You have so much to learn about me, love. Remember when I put that concealment shield around us when we were at the lake?"

Her pretty kissable mouth opened. "Yes. Are you saying we're in a bubble now?"

"I am. If anyone happens to walk up to the hot spring, I've made it look like a dark ugly pool. No one will disturb us."

Tory pushed off the side of the pool, tugged him away from the edge, and straddled him. "What other talents do you possess, Mr. Forrester?"

He nibbled her chin down to her neck and then dragged his tongue up to her ear, not quite giving his mate what she wanted. "I'd rather show you a little each day until the end of time."

She chuckled. "You are such a tease."

He ran his hands down her waist, enjoying the feel of her curves, as heat seared his insides. Kenton wanted this experience to be about enjoying his mate, but sometimes his desires overwhelmed him to the point where he had to make love to her.

With her body pressed hard against his dick, Kenton needed her lips on his. Tory cupped his face and returned the kiss with matching passion. This was where he needed to be. With a flick of his hand, their bathing suits disappeared.

"I love that trick," Tory said. "You'll have to show me how you do that later. Right now, I have other things on my mind."

"I love that we always seem to want the same thing," he said as he nibbled on her bottom lip.

She reached between them, and when she grabbed his cock, lightning bolts of need and desire shot up his spine with more power than anything he'd ever experienced. Every cell in his body was screaming for him to take her.

He cupped her head with one hand, and her back with the other. The kiss that followed made him want to give his kingdom to the gods of Fate—or to the Four Sisters—assuming they were responsible for this amazing woman coming into his life.

Tory and he did a dance with their tongues that bordered on indecent erotic lust. When he couldn't take it any longer, he leaned back. "I need more."

"Then take it." Tory grinned.

He swept his hand over the water between them, forcing the fluid away. With Tory's bare breasts exposed, he pounced.

"How did you do that?" she asked.

"It's all magic, love," he telepathed, because he was a tad too busy to talk.

He suckled one breast while he plucked the nipple of the other with his fingers. Every touch set him on fire. Maybe making love in already heated water might not be the best idea though, since he wanted to explore all of her.

While he could always teleport them to the two lounge chairs next to the hot spring, her moans and his groans might alert some unwanted company. With that in mind, he glanced at their clothes that he teleported to the towel rack in his bathroom. Finally, he pictured his bed at his cabin and took Tory there.

Tory clasped his shoulders. "Why did we leave the hot springs?"

"If you're disappointed, we can go back."

"No. I'm just surprised, that's all. I thought you said you'd warn me the next time you took me out of my current space. That will cost you, you know."

If she hadn't been fighting a smile, he might have been worried. "I will take all the punishment you see fit to dole out. But hurry. I don't think I can wait much longer."

Tory chuckled and then pressed on his shoulder to indicate she wanted him on his back. Kenton obliged. With quick reflexes, she jumped to her knees and placed one leg between his and then wedged the other leg in there, too. She grabbed his dick. Instinct made him take hold of her wrist.

She grinned and then went down on him. Her breasts were within easy reach, so he gently massaged them. The combination of touching her soft skin, together with what she was doing to him, was almost too much to handle. In fact, a second later, his cum shot straight into her mouth. Drat. He hadn't meant to lose control.

Tory sat up. "Someone's easy."

Kenton loved nothing more than a good challenge. "Let's see how long you last."

"That was my plan all along." Tory lifted a self-satisfied chin.

He tossed her onto her back and then slid between her legs. There would be no mercy tonight. Kenton spread her legs wide and then licked her clit before gently flicking his tongue across it in rapid succession.

Tory moaned and grabbed his shoulders, her scales flashing an increasing brighter yellow with each swipe. Having a visual barometer of her emotions was amazing. Not that he couldn't sense how turned on she was, seeing it was just as much of a high. The more he nipped and licked, the faster she moved her hips from side to side.

"Kenton," she moaned. "Please, I need you to fill me."

Tory was his mate. His woman. And he promised himself right then and there to love and cherish her until the end of time. "As you wish."

Kenton pressed his chest to hers and kissed her as he slid right into her slick opening. Tory sucked in a deep breath and then wrapped her legs around his waist. As if she'd put a magic spell on him, time and distance ceased to exist as she met him thrust for thrust. Her scales flashed, and her inner light glowed. Her blonde hair made her purple and gold irises stand out even more. But it wasn't just her beauty that had captured him. It was her strength, her resiliency, and her selfless desire to help others.

She pulled his head toward hers and kissed him. Her sharpened teeth could have drawn blood, but Tory was gentle. When she broke the kiss and dragged her mouth to his neck, he was ready.

"Now, my love," he telepathed.

He barely felt the bite, but his hormones sure jacked up something fierce. Tory opened her mouth and let out a primal scream. A second later, he came hard. His skin pulsed, and his heart throbbed. There was nowhere in this realm he'd rather be.

"I love you, Kenton Forrester."

"I love you even more, my love."

Kenton rolled over and dragged her on top. With her hair spread over his chest, her breasts against his skin, and one hand stroking his shoulder, it convinced him that he was the luckiest man in any realm.

Kenton gently lifted Tory off of him so he could teleport to the bathroom for a wet towel to clean them up with. When he returned the towel to the bathroom, he checked that their clothes were dry. He then carried them out and placed them on the bed.

"Want to try putting them on without using your hands?" he asked.

"How do I do that?"

"Close your eyes, picture the clothes on your body, and then swipe your hand like this." He moved a few of his fingers in a rather specific pattern, hoping she could copy it.

"I'll try."

Tory did as he asked, but the finger movement was a bit off. She ended up with most of her clothes on her body, except that Tory was wearing his shirt. Thank goodness, her top didn't end up on him— not that it would fit.

She opened her eyes, looked down, and grinned. "Did I do that?"

He loved how excited she was after each success. "If I had helped, trust me, I wouldn't have given you any other clothes but my shirt to wear. So yes, it was all you."

Kenton pulled her to his chest and kissed her. "Life with you is going to be fun."

"I couldn't agree more."

"ARE YOU READY for this?" Tory asked.

Kenton's mouth slightly opened. "Why wouldn't I be? We're just visiting your sister and her new baby."

"No one in your family has kids, do they?" Tory didn't want him to be uncomfortable.

"No, but it's not like I'm afraid Sapphire will attack me." He reached over and tickled Tory.

She grabbed his hands. "Stop," she said, laughing almost too hard to talk.

Kenton straightened. "Fly or teleport?" he asked.

They were at her house, because the cell reception in the forest was intermittent at best. "How about we drive? It's not far. That way, you can get the lay of the land so you'll know where it would be safe to land in the future." She had high hopes, he'd learn to shift into a dragon at some point.

He tapped her nose. "As soon as Poppy trains you, I bet you'll never take to the skies again."

"That would be like you never using any of your magic."

"Oh. I guess we have a lot to learn about each other then," Kenton said.

"We do." Tory picked up her car keys. "Ready?"

"Yup."

At the car, she dangled them. "Do you want to drive?"

He laughed. "You haven't figured out yet that I don't know how to drive?"

Now he was stalling. "What are you talking about?"

He explained how he'd used magic the first time. "I never touched my foot to the pedals."

At first, she wasn't sure if she believed him, but it made sense. Why learn to drive if he could teleport? Tory closed her fist over the keys. "Into the passenger seat, buddy."

Kenton laughed, and she fell a little more in love with him. When they arrived at Kaleena's condo, they took the elevator to her floor. Yes, they could have teleported, but if they'd just appeared out of thin air and a tenant saw them, it could create quite a stir.

Tory knocked and Finn answered. He grinned and then nodded to Kenton. "Come in."

Kaleena came out of the bedroom carrying their precious bundle, and Tory rushed over to her niece. "She's so big!"

"It's amazing how fast she is growing. Do you want to hold her?" her sister asked.

"Absolutely."

Tory carefully held the wide-eyed baby as she walked over to the sofa and sat down. Kenton sat next to her, his gaze on the child. With everything that had gone on, they hadn't had time to discuss having a family, but she bet they would soon.

"We have something to ask you," Tory said.

"If you want to keep Sapphire," Kaleena said. "The answer is no."

Tory laughed. "That's not it, though I would love to have a child like this."

Kenton squeezed her leg. *"That can be arranged—or rather we can work on that if you'd like?"* he telepathed.

This was not the place for that conversation. "Kenton, maybe you'd like to explain."

"Sure. I hope Tory told you that my father is the King of Feyrion?"

"She did."

"Someday—though no one knows exactly when that will be—my parents will step down, and I will be king. Tory, naturally, will become queen."

All cheer evaporated from Kaleena's face. "Is this where you tell me you're moving to Feyrion?" she asked.

"No. Kenton needs to be here for now to watch over the portals, and besides, I am a Guardian. I belong here. Hopefully, I won't be needed on Feyrion until after Sapphire and my other niece can take my place." She wasn't sure if that was possible, but Tory didn't want to think she'd be leaving her family any time soon.

"I'm glad."

"That brings us to our upcoming celebration," Kenton said. "My parents want to host a kind of happy mating party for Tory and me on Feyrion. We'd like you three to come."

The sparkle in Kaleena's eyes returned. "We'd love to. Right, Finn?"

"Are you kidding? How many people in this universe get to see three different realms?"

"Very few, I bet," Kenton said.

Chapter Twenty-Six

TORY COULDN'T BELIEVE she was on top of the mountain learning how to teleport, especially since their grand coming out party was in a few days. Kenton had agreed to join her and Poppy since he teleported more often than she did.

"You've teleported a few times before, so this shouldn't be too hard," Poppy said. "Kenton, would you go over to that large tree please?"

One minute he was standing next to her, and the next, he was by the tree.

Tory faced Poppy. "Now what?"

"When you have the end point in sight, it's fairly easy. Focus on where you want to go, and just will your body to go there. Ready?" Poppy asked.

"Yes." Tory inhaled and then turned her full attention to Kenton. *Move.*

One second she was next to Poppy and the next she was with Kenton. The part she wasn't sure she'd get used to was that she didn't even feel any sensation of speed.

He grabbed hold of her and lifted her up. "You did it! I knew you could."

Tory laughed. "Poppy said that was the easy part."

"Hey, appreciate all victories. Even the small ones. Now return to her."

Tory turned around, kept her gaze on Poppy and teleported there. Once more she succeeded.

"Now for something more challenging."

For the next three hours, Poppy threw test after test at her. Any time Tory failed, Kenton found her, bolstered her spirits, and helped her find her destination. Finally, Tory sat on the ground. "I think my brain is fried."

Kenton and Poppy laughed. "Teleporting takes mental energy."

Her mate stroked her head. "Like remaining invisible, but with practice you'll improve."

She looked up at him and clasped his hand. "I hope so."

"Ready to head back to town?" he asked.

"I'm ready for bed." She didn't want to whine, but every cell in her body lacked energy.

"Do you mind if we stop at Angelique's coffee shop first?"

"Sure, but why?"

"I need to tell her that I no longer have time to be the best coffee server in town."

"Aw. I'll miss you at lunch." Tory threw him a pout.

"During your lunch break, you can return to the cabin. It will only take you a second to get from the jewelry store to the woods."

"Ahem. Let's limit our talk of our sexual desires to when we telepath, okay?" Tory asked.

Kenton grinned. *"I'm sure everyone knows what I'm thinking."*

Tory punched him in the arm and then let Kenton help her up. Tory faced Poppy. "You are the best. I promise I will continue to practice until I master this. Faced with not being able to touch my mate during my lunch break, I am even more determined to be the best teleporter in Edendale."

They all laughed. Kenton then grabbed her hand. Next thing she knew, she was in the alley behind Angelique's. "Mind if we have a coffee and a pastry first before you break her heart?" Tory asked.

"You bet. Anything for you, love."

"DID YOU SEE my mother and father yet?" Tory asked as she peered out the big picture window of one of the palace suites that overlooked the expansive backyard.

This was turning out to be a bigger event than she'd imagined. Kenton's mother must have had fifty people working to make this party perfect. That or Queen Arianna had merely swiped her hand and the tables set up themselves.

Kenton moved behind Tory and placed his hands on her shoulders. "Yes. Everyone is here. It will be epic."

Tory looked at everyone milling around, drinking, eating, and laughing. "Shouldn't we be out there?"

He turned her around. "Think of it as a wedding of sorts. When all of the guests have arrived, my mother and father will take their place on the platform and announce us."

"Cool. I'll be ready." She looked down at her dress. It was a knee length pale yellow silk dress with swirls of black interwoven throughout. It was exquisite. His mother had picked it out. "Let me ask you. Do these colors and patterns represent my dragon scale colors?"

Kenton smiled. "It does. And the jewels in your hair are ones that represent my family's heritage."

"They look like the Orlandan jewels similar to the ones on my bracelet that you gave me."

"They are. Now that we can communicate, you don't have to wear it if you don't want to."

"But I want to wear it. To me, it represents you."

Kenton pulled her into an embrace and hugged her. "I love you more than life itself, my sweet dragon shifter," he whispered a second before he kissed her.

I love you too. You are my everything. Not wanting to break the kiss, she'd telepathed it.

The kiss intensified, and every part of her body flashed, pulsed, and soared.

"Ahem. We're ready for you," Meena said.

Heat raced up Tory's face as she broke the kiss. Kenton turned to his sister. "You did that on purpose, didn't you?"

Meena grinned and gave a shrug.

Kenton laughed and then turned back to Tory. "Ready?"

"All I have to do is walk down what might be called an aisle and face your parents?"

"We can teleport there if you wish?"

Decisions, decisions. "Walking will give me time to check out the crowd."

"That's my girl."

Together, they made their way outside. His parents were seated in thrones that were hand carved from a black wood. Because jewels of all sorts were encrusted in the wood, Tory didn't want to think what that must have cost.

Kenton placed a hand on her back and then led her down the aisle. Rows of chairs had suddenly appeared as soon as they stepped out. Where the tables of food went, she had no idea. Welcome to the world of magic.

A harpist, who was sitting off to the side, strummed her instrument. The music sounded quite ethereal, which she suspected was on purpose. Tory's mom and dad were both grinning, looking healthy and happy. Without being too obvious, Tory looked for Danita and Griffin but didn't spot them. She did see Poppy, her baby, and a man who she guessed was her mate. Oh, my. She'd done well for herself. Good for Poppy.

How incredible of the Forresters to allow so many from Tarradon to share in their world. The level of trust amazed her. Only now did she fully understand why there was need for secrecy. This world was so very special.

When they reached the podium, Kenton turned her around. Wow. Hundreds of people were there, but she only recognized a few. She never did ask Kenton how many people lived in this realm, but she suspected there were a lot.

Kenton held up his hand. "I want to thank all of you for being here on this wonderful occasion. I never thought I would ever find a mate who matches me wit for wit, but Tory Sinclair is everything I'd dreamed about and more. Someday, she will be our queen."

The crowd clapped, and Tory wanted to teleport out of there—but of course, she didn't dare. While it might be tens or hundreds of years before she became queen, this was as grand as any coronation she'd read about.

"Should I say something?" Tory telepathed.

"If you wish."

That was not the answer she was looking for, but she wanted to honor his family. "I can't tell you all how amazing it is to be here. Feyrion is such a beautiful and magical place that has already stolen my heart." The crowd sighed. "After my near-death experience that prompted Kenton to give me a piece of his life light, we became connected on a molecular level. He has been true to me every moment of every day. While I still think he should get a cell phone, I wouldn't change anything about my man."

The crowd laughed and then clapped.

King Leighton and Queen Arianna stepped next to them. "Let's enjoy the day and celebrate the new addition to our family," the queen said. She hugged Tory. *"I couldn't have picked anyone better for my son,"* she telepathed.

"Thank you," Tory said out loud.

The people stood, and as they moved to the end of the aisle, the chairs disappeared and the tables filled with food returned. Tory wasn't sure she'd ever get used to that. For now, she'd accept it all. If her ability to do this kind of thing became commonplace, she might have a hard time not lapsing into magic on Tarradon, and that would be hard to explain.

"Ready to meet the masses, love?"

She sighed and then wrapped her arms around his neck. "What did I do to deserve such a remarkable man as you?"

"You were born beautiful, kind, generous, and incredible yourself."

Tory's heart melted. Oh my, life with Kenton Forrester was going to be absolutely amazing.

I hope you enjoyed reading Tory and Kenton's story
as much as I enjoyed writing it.

Don't forget to sign up for my newsletter *to receive some free books, as well as up-to-date information on my stories. If you prefer to only receive notices regarding my releases, follow me on BookBub.*

http://smarturl.it/VellaDayNL
bookbub.com/authors/vella-day

THE END

HIDDEN REALMS OF SILVER LAKE (Paranormal)

Awakened By Flames (book 1)

Seduced By Flames (book 2)

Kissed By Flames (book 3)

Destiny In Flames (book 4)

Box Set (books 1-4)

Passionate Flames (book 5)

Ignited By Flames (book 6)

Touched By Flames (book 7)

Box Set (books 5-7)

Bound By Flames (book 8)

Fueled By Flames (book 9)

FOUR SISTERS OF FATE: HIDDEN REALMS OF SILVER LAKE (Paranormal)

Poppy (book 1)

Primrose (book 2)

Acacia (book 3)

Magnolia (book 4)

Box Set (books 1-4)

Jace (book 5)

Tanner (book 6)

WERES AND WITCHES OF SILVER LAKE (Paranormal)

A Magical Shift (book 1)

Catching Her Bear (book 2)

Surge of Magic (book 3)

The Bear's Forbidden Wolf (book 4)

Her Reluctant Bear (book 5)

Freeing His Tiger (book 6)

Protecting His Wolf (book 7)

Waking His Bear (book 8)

Melting Her Wolf's Heart (book 9)

Her Wolf's Guarded Heart (book 10)

His Rogue Bear (book 11)

Box Set (books 1-4)

Box Set (books 5-8)

Reawakening Their Bears (book 12)

PACK WARS (Paranormal)

Training Their Mate (book 1)

Claiming Their Mate (book 2)

Rescuing Their Virgin Mate (book 3)

Box Set (books 1-3)

Loving Their Vixen Mate (book 4)

Fighting For Their Mate (book 5)

Enticing Their Mate (book 6)

Box Set (books 1-4)

Complete Box Set (books 1-6)

HIDDEN HILLS SHIFTERS (Paranormal)

An Unexpected Diversion (book 1)

Bare Instincts (book 2)

Shifting Destinies (book 3)

Embracing Fate (book 4)

Promises Unbroken (book 5)

Bare 'N Dirty (book 6)

Hidden Hills Shifters Complete Box Set (books 1-6)

MONTANA PROMISES (Full length contemporary)

Promises of Mercy (book 1)

Foundations For Three (book 2)

Montana Fire (book 3)

Montana Promises Box Set (books 1-3)

Hart To Hart (Book 4)

Burning Seduction (Book 5)

Montana Promises Complete Box Set (books 1-5)

ROCK HARD, MONTANA (contemporary novellas)

Montana Desire (book 1)

Awakening Passions (book 2)

PLEDGED TO PROTECT (contemporary romantic suspense)

From Panic To Passion (book 1)

From Danger To Desire (book 2)

From Terror To Temptation (book 3)

Pledged To Protect Box Set (books 1-3)

BURIED SERIES (contemporary romantic suspense)

Buried Alive (book 1)

Buried Secrets (book 2)

Buried Deep (book 3)

The Buried Series Complete Box Set (books 1-3)

A NASH MYSTERY (Contemporary)

Sidearms and Silk(book 1)

Black Ops and Lingerie(book 2)

A Nash Mystery Box Set (books 1-2)

STARTER SETS

Contemporary

Paranormal

Author Bio

Want three FREE books? Sign up for my newsletter and receive MONTANA DESIRE, AN UNEXPECTED DIVERSION, and BARE INSTINCTS.
COPY AND PASTE INTO YOUR BROWSER:
http://smarturl.it/o4cz93?IQid=MLite

Not only do I love to read, write, and dream, I'm an extrovert. I enjoy being around people and am always trying to understand what makes them tick. Not only must my books have a happily ever after, I need characters I can relate to. My men are wonderful, dynamic, smart, strong, and the best lovers in the world (of course).

I believe I am the luckiest woman. I do what I love and I have a wonderful, supportive husband, who happens to be hot!

Fun facts about me

(1) I'm a math nerd who loves spreadsheets. Give me numbers and I'll find a pattern.

(2) I live on a Costa Rica beach!

(3) I also like to exercise. Yes, I know I'm odd.

I love hearing from readers either on FB or via email (hint, hint).

Social Media Sites

Website:
www.velladay.com

FB:
facebook.com/vella.day.90

Twitter:
@velladay4

Gmail:
velladayauthor@gmail.com

Instagram:
@dayvella